Suddenly in Love in Paris

By: Humberto Páez and Carmen Castellanos Soto

Whit enjoyment and respect for your acquisition of this book;

To: _____

Our lives become easier when we simply turn a page and start a new chapter.

Humberto and Carmen

Prologue

The events described in this story take place between the years 1950 and 2016.

In this book you will find situations that reflect the story of two people –a man and a woman– that meet in the Golden Years and start a new life, full of lovely experiences. They go through moments of happiness and sadness during their relationship. These moments can be experienced at any adult age such as the feelings of love and passion of these characters. Such feelings can be experienced by any healthy couple.

We recommend that you practice the demonstrations of love expressed in this book and also recommend a change of setting such as traveling and vacationing as a couple.

Likewise, in this book we expose situations and problems which are common in our daily lives and we express situations that are in accordance with its title.

The end of the book is quite amusing.

CHAPTER I
BALTIMORE, MARYLAND 1948, LOOKING FOR FORTUNE

It was the year 1948, when Mr. Richard Smith left his wife and little son, Christopher, behind in the State of Maryland, leaving for Cuba in the hope that the existing rumors of being able to invest in a gas station were true. He hoped to establish his life in Cuba once he had reunited with his family. His friends had mentioned that there were many possibilities of establishing a prosperous business in Cuba.

It was not easy separating from his family, but, he had to take advantage of the times as there were possibilities for foreigners to exploit an island rich in many aspects; where the dollar and the Cuban currency were of equal value. Richard had left extremely worried; preoccupied in leaving behind his family in a difficult monetary condition, but he had given his wife some money he had saved, so that they could survive until he was able to establish his business and send them money from Cuba, and finally bring them to live with him in the island.

After having traveled through the entire island of Cuba, the place that he found more suitable for his investment and establishing the business was in Matanzas. There was a big movement of vehicles in that province, because there were several tourist places, such as Varadero Beach, Yumuri Valley, the Bellamar Caves and the Canimar Bridge among many other attractions.

With the small capital that he took with him and a loan that he obtained from an American bank, which had a branch in Cuba, he was able to open up a gas station, that also had a mechanic shop to change oil in cars, as well as providing for the cleaning of vehicles and tire repairs. This service center became the most modern in the province of Matanzas. The construction took approximately 18 months. Once finished, Richard went to Maryland to bring his wife and his son with him for the opening of the business and to move permanently to Cuba.

In the year 1950, Richard Smith (Ricky as his friends called him) was totally established, his wife Nancy was the cashier and bookkeeper but if it was necessary she would also pump gas, plus two more employees, a native guy of dark complexion who was in charge of oiling the vehicles and the other employee who was a native that fixed the tires and cleaned the vehicles.

Little Christopher would go to the service center after school and put all of his attention in the management of the business. He was only four years old and was willing to help his father in the business.

The business was prosperous in a very short time, Christopher was growing and was fluent in both languages, English and Spanish. Since he was a very modest person, he was not able to distinguish people by class or race and interacted the same way with everybody. On or about 1955, his wife got pregnant and gave birth to a girl in her home town of Maryland. This girl was named Christine but her nickname was Christy.

It was the year 1956 when the political differences in Cuba were felt by population. The beginning of the revolution by rebels against the Government started in the Orient Province.

In 1953, a group of opponents of the reigning government arose against the army of the reigning President, attacking the Moncada Base in Oriente Province; occurring on July 26th. The group leader was Fidel Castro Ruz, who, in 1955, after having been in jail because of an indictment, named the guerilla movement "July 26".

The opposing force began advancing towards the capital, Havana, and during the early hours of the first day of January 1959, the president with his advisors boarded an airplane and left the country, leaving Cuba under the rebel government directed by Fidel Castro.

CHAPTER II
REMEMBRANCES BY CHRISTOPHER

In 1960 the United States had severed all political relations with Cuba and all American industries had been intervened by the Cuban government. Two agents of the Cuban government took possession of Mr. Richard Smith's business. He was not allowed to enter his business and the doors were sealed; it was then that the family decided that they had to leave Cuba as soon as possible.

I Christopher Smith, am approximately 15 years old and I am perfectly fluent in both languages, English and Spanish, and I am able to see the suffering of my parents, who after building a great business with a lot of effort, grew accustomed to living on the island. We love Cuba as if it was our own country.

My parents were permanent residents on the island, but, some of the capital they had earned was in the United States, because they were advised by friends abroad that they should have some money in the United States. Because of this they invested in gold bonds and they were able to get this money out of the country in time. This helped them start a new life in the United States, where a big important tire business was established. They helped both of the employees they had in Cuba leave their country and flee to the United States, since they were trustworthy people and very good in the management of the business.

I had to continue studying in Maryland, and helping in the business after school. I finished high school and was unable to study a career precisely because I had to help my father, who was already very sick and I had to take control of the business. Afterwards, I became an international business man. When Christopher arrived in the United States ten years later, he had memories from his life in

Cuba and it was pretty difficult for him to get used to the way of life in the United States. He was back in his country and of Irish descendant, but, those 10 years that he lived in Cuba, he grew accustomed to Spanish and he was completely fluent in that language. When he started going to school in Maryland it was not easy studying in his native language. He never stopped communicating in English with his parents, but he felt like an immigrant in his own land because his classmates constantly made fun of his grammar. It was all new to him, the streets, the buildings, traffic, the food, wandering alone; he missed having left all his friends behind. They played alone in the streets of Matanzas, going to the park, fishing and going to the movies. Life was problem-free. Now, he had to go out with his parents and his sister everywhere, who also missed the land they left behind. He did not feel well, he felt like a bird trapped in a big cage.

When I turned 30 years old I abandoned my bohemian life and married a very pretty girl, a blonde girl with blue eyes that I met at my business and I was captivated by her looks. She came to my business for car service. I personally attended the girl, which I did not use to do and I was rather courteous in calling her attention. When she was giving me her identification to prepare her statement and issue a warranty, I took down her home address and telephone number. That same night I drove by her house to know what type of neighborhood she lived in. It was a middle class neighborhood and I observed that there was a car parked out of the house with a sign of a Plummer, with the same telephone number in her statement. I called the number and an older gentleman answered the phone. I thought it had to be her father because she was too young to be married.

I waited until the following morning to make sure the man who answered had left their home to work and to find out if she would be answering the phone. It was just like I had figured. When she answered I immediately recognized her voice as if I had known her all my life. I introduced myself and she told me that I was fresh for using her personal information for my personal interests. This was surprising and I lost my voice. For a second I lost all interest in insisting, but, I was not going to give up and let pass what I felt for her and I called again and she answered. I asked her not to hang up on me and to let me talk.

—What do you want?

—Invite you to an ice cream shop close to your house.

—Why do you want to have ice cream with me.

—Because I like you a lot as a woman and would like to be your friend.

—I don't know. I will call you at work later. What is your name?

—I was prompt to answer, Christopher.

—Only Christopher.

—Yes, I told her, I am the only Christopher in that business. I am the owner.

Every time the phone rang I ran to answer in case it was her, five hours passed and I thought she would never call. Then, a few minutes before closing the phone rang and I didn't answer. I asked my attendant to take the call, she told me it was a woman and that she was calling for me. I ran into a chair, a couple of things fell from my desk and I answered, agitated and nervous.

—Hello, Hello, who is it?

—Kathy

—Let me know if we are going to the ice cream shop.

—When?

—Right now.

—Where do I pick you up?

—No, I'll meet you there. I am going in my car.

When I got to the ice cream shop I was looking for her.

I had her next to me and I couldn't see her. Then, she asked me.

—Are you looking for me, Christopher?

—I had not seen you. What a surprise! Thank you for coming. Do you want to sit inside of the ice cream shop, or in one of the cars where we can get served?

—Are you crazy, my parents would kill me, it is better if we have the ice cream inside. I answered.

—OK! While we had the ice cream I didn't take my eyes off her and observed her, at a time she looked at me and noticed that I had not eaten my ice cream.

—You invited me to have ice cream and you haven't eaten a thing.

—Do you have a boyfriend?

—No, and you? Do you have a girlfriend?

—Not me.

—Are you sure you don't have a girlfriend?

—No, no, no. (She did not insist anymore).

—Well, it is ok, if you say so, I believe it.

When she went to get the ice cream, he touched her hand and she took her hand away from him immediately and asked him.

—What are you doing touching my hand?

—I wanted to touch the hand of a doll.

—I am not a doll, I am Kathy.

She was very firm when she answered. All of a sudden I decided to ask her and I did:

—Do you want to be my girlfriend?

She avoided the answer.

—You invited me to have ice cream and to be your friend. Not your girlfriend and added:

—I have to leave now.

Since we had only been together for 15 minutes I asked her:

—Why do you have to leave so soon?

—I have to leave soon because my father is about to get home and I don't want to be late?

—Do I see you tomorrow?

She answered that she was not sure, then I told her to call me when she wanted to go out with me again.

That day I went home very happy, whistling and with a big smile, my mother asked me why I was so happy. What happened? Oh God, this kid is flirting with another women again.

The next day I went back to my duties, but my mind was on anything but my obligations. I was thinking if she would call me back or not, or, if I should call her again. Then 10 minutes before the closing of the business the phone rang and I answered, Kathy and I exchanged a few words and we met at the same place and it was successively like that, until we finally had formed a relationship. There was a difference in age because I was 30 years old and she was 23. I was never tired of looking at her, her eyes and her hair was so blonde. It looked like golden threads, her features were very refined and I admired her elegant and educated manners even though she was not a high class person.

We used to go out to wander around her house since she was not used to going out in a car with a man since at this time society was very conservative. She had never had a fiancé, only admirers from school. Kathy was a virgin. One day when we were walking by the park, near her house, I introduced my hand in her breast and she slapped my face. I was astonished of her reaction knowing that she had been brought up by her family under an old traditional system. I was surprised because it was a time where there were many girls into intimate relationship with boyfriends at an early age.

After several months she asked about my intentions with her since we had to formalize our relationship as her parents were not happy that she was so often out of house escaping to the park to meet with him. It was necessary that he meet her parents and talk about marriage. Kathy was their daughter and her parents were very jealous of her.

The day came when he had to go to her house to meet her parents and have a talk with them. As soon as I met her father he went straight to the point and told me that I could be very wealthy but his house was a very respectful house. Then I told him that I was in love with her and that my intentions were to marry his daughter. Not even ninety days had elapsed when there was a family meeting, actually it took place on Thanksgiving Day (a religious meal to thank God for the bounties received during the year). The reception took place at my home, then I proposed to her on my knees and gave her the ring. We immediately started looking for an apartment to buy and remodel; neither one of us wanted to live with our parents.

We married six months after that reception at St. Patricks Church in Baltimore, Maryland. It was a day in May, it was all very pretty and with lots of flowers. Approximately 100 people attended the wedding at the church, among family members, there were friends and employees from my business.

When I saw her walking into the church accompanied by her father and holding his arm, she looked like an angel dressed in white. Behind them two children entered with the rings and the flowers. My parents were crying of emotion and happiness as well as her parents. My parents were praising God because my head was finally settling down and I didn't go from one woman to the other.

The reception took place in my home in the garden. The honeymoon was in New Orleans and we stayed at a very old hotel "The Columns Hotel" in the Garden District, a beautiful hotel. The bedroom was very antique and the shower was an old high bathtub. When we went to bed to consummate our marriage our legs were above our heads because the floor was sunken. The elevator was driven by an elevator operator and was closed with iron bar doors. The room had a private terrace facing the street where the tram went by constantly. The trees were full of necklaces of multiple colors from a party that is celebrated every year in March, the famous "Mardi Gras". There was jazz every night, romantic music from the bar on the front porch.

We took tours of two cemeteries, and a boat on the Mississippi River. We also took some other famous tours. The tour that made Kathy uncomfortable was the night that we walked through the "French Quarter". At midnight there were many of people that had drunk too much; some were disguised and some of the women that were staying at the hotels would go out onto balconies and pulling their shirts up and showed off their breasts. I wanted to bother Kathy and I told her that I took her to New Orleans for precisely the reason. She was crying when she turned back to me and saying:

—You are crazy, what type of proposal is that?

—I explained that I was kidding. How can I ask you to show your breasts, when those are only mine?

We also went to the most famous coffee shop in most cities of the world "Café Du Monde", where we had coffee sitting under the stars in the French Quarter, where the famous doughnuts known as "Beighnets" were served. We also visited St. Luis Cathedral, a beautiful structure. After that we went to the famous sugar cane plantations. We drove approximately five hours to get to the Plantations, where we spent an additional five hours in one of them. It was the property of a family that had such a sad story that Kathy was dying to leave. She saw too many graves in the yard of the property.

The whole family including the children died of Tuberculosis and she urged us to leave that place.

We spent seven days of honeymoon in New Orleans and walked so much that we had lost some weight.

CHAPTER III
AFTER THE HONEYMOON

After the honeymoon we went back to work, I brought her to work with me. Every day we were closer, in work as well as in personal affairs. She was anxious to have a child, but it did not happen until we had been married for three years. Kathy got pregnant and had a girl, we named that girl "Milam". She was a very happy and large girl. The grandparents were crazy about holding her and playing with her. They fell in love with her smile and the two dimples, one on each cheek that formed when she smiled. She was born in April and she had a strong will and a lot of personality, even as a baby.

After that, when Milam was already four years old, we had a son, whom we named "Richard" after my father. We called him Ricky and he was a disaster, he wouldn't leave anything alone, touching everything, breaking decorations and after laughing. When he turned one year old my father died, it was very sad and a great loss for all of us. He was the best head of family and a great businessman.

We had to purchase a house in my mother's neighborhood because the apartment was already small for all of us.

In addition, to the distribution of tires I started a real estate investment business because there was a lot of competition in the tire distribution and there was a big competition between the companies that diminished the sales. I formed a real estate investment business, becoming a developer and started constructing apartment buildings. At one point I had 220 apartments in different areas of the city.

We had everything to be happy: wealth, health, love

and faith, but, it got to a point that the business absorbed our lives and we did not even have time to spend on vacation with the children and we even missed regular family outings.

When Milam turned 15 years old, Kathy got pregnant again this time without planning it, since neither of us favored abortion, we had the child. Her name was Jacqueline. "Jacky" brought back the happiness that we were lacking since my father's death. We were only dedicated to work and obligations.

When Jacky was ten years old, my wife had an accident, because of a rush, she made the mistake of passing by a stop sign. A truck hit her from the side and killed the girl at the scene of the accident. I had a heart attack when I was informed of the accident, though I did not know it. It happened due to the pain of the loss of my child. After the tragedy my wife fell into a crisis because she felt guilty and I took her to the best Psychologists and Psychiatrists, but she could not fight the depression and stopped working. I took her to her parents' house, who were very old, thinking that she would get better, nevertheless it didn't work.

I received a call one morning. My mother was living with me at the time with the help of a maid. Between the two of us we took care of the children. It was approximately 6:30 in the morning. That call changed the pace of my life. My wife's mother crying and screaming told me that Kathy was dead. I immediately went there and found a police car, a car from the homicides department and an ambulance. My eyes couldn't believe what I saw. My mother-in-law told me that she had poisoned herself with several sleeping pills, my heart stopped. It was not possible that the girl that I met who was a hard working and happy girl, would have such a tragic ending and leaving me with my two children. Her parents were very sad and died in a period of two years after they lost their daughter.

Two years have passed; I had lost my mother five years ago and I have lived a very quiet life, with my children and without a lover. My children were already fully grown. I have been directing both businesses. Milam is a lawyer now and practices real estate and Ricky graduated with a degree in Business Administration. I left both businesses under the supervision and control of my children. I only directed the business in my capacity as president of both companies. I was feeling extremely sad thinking about the course that my life had taken, when I always expected to spend my last years with my wife who was the love of my life. Also, I was always thinking about the loss of my little daughter and I felt very lonely in that big house. All of these thoughts made me think about enjoying my life a little bit more and the first thing I planned without thinking too much about it and did it, was buying a ticket to Europe and took a two-week vacation.

My children thought it was a great idea and two months after that I saw myself on a flight to Paris.

CHAPTER IV
FOUND LOVE AT 60 IN PARIS

The French Airlines called all first class passengers to board the plane, —Monsieur, here is your sit —said the Stewardess. I was in the place I had asked for when I made the reservation, by the window. It began taking off and when it was approximately two thousand feet more or less high I looked down and saw the city where I was born, where I married and had my children, the tears ran down my cheeks. My wife's dream was traveling to France and because of the urge to make money I never gave her the pleasure of going on that trip.

In a short time, we were over the Atlantic Ocean, I could see the sea from the airplane. There was a television set in front of me on the airplane and it was showing a very pretty love movie named, "The Bridges of Madison County", the main characters of the movie are Clint Eastwood and Meryl Streep, two of Hollywood's top stars.

By my side was a well-known movie star, Mike Benitez, who is a comedian. We were chatting for a long time. There was also a retired politician with his wife with whom I also had a long conversation. I couldn't fall sleep because I was kind of nervous as I don't like flying. I was awake at lunch time because a Stewardess woke me up.

We were only two hours away from our destination, descending into Charles De Gaulle's Airport in Paris. When we were approaching landing I could see Paris from my window. I saw how beautiful it was, I could distinguish the Eiffel Tower with its amusement park and the variety of roofs and different types of castles. As we kept approaching Paris I could see the roads and the buildings until the airplane had totally descended.

I took a taxi, which is called "fiacre" in French and

went straight to the hotel "Reinassance Paris Vendome", situated in the street named Mont Tabor, it was a five-star hotel at that time.

As soon as I got to the hotel, I took a shower and went to bed. I was very tired and it was already night time when I woke up. The difference in time made me feel disoriented. I went to the restaurant in the hotel, for the first time I ate an original French Dinner, Duck marinated with Orange, accompanied by Crepes with spinach and a special cream. The restaurant was very elegant with contemporary decorations, it had a wooden floor. It was formal and my suite was very pretty and comfortable, it was distributed as follows: living room, a den used as an office, the bedroom with two balconies facing the street, with a small table to eat in or have breakfast and a bathroom. The service was great and the personnel was courteous and respectful. I went back to sleep early because I was tired because of the stress of the trip.

I woke up to a beautiful sunny day and I decided to take a taxi for a ride through the center of the city. Around 10:00 I was hungry and decided to look for a bakery to have a French Pie and Coffee. I saw a bakery with tables inside and outside of the shop, under the sun. It was the month of March 2006. I went to the counter and asked for an express coffee and a pastry that I saw through the window, I was pointing at the pastry and asking for the coffee at the same time. The employee did not understand my English, then again I asked in Spanish and she kept saying a long phrase that I did not understand at all. I got desperate because I was very tense and started talking to her in a very high tone, telling her:

—What language do I have to use, Chinese?

—The girl smiled and told me: Qu' est que vous voulez

monsieur?

I internally thought and remembered all of her ascendants and started screaming:

—Express coffee, express, express.

Then a voice that was coming from a nearby table, asked me:

—Mister, can I help you?

—I turned and asked her:

—Do you work here?

She answered:

—No, I am here to have a snack with some friends.

Christoper then told her, please can you tell the girl in the counter that I want a pastry I saw in the window and coffee and I offered and asked if she would like something to eat that I would invite her.

I made this gesture being greatful but she turned to the girl and told her:

—"Un café au lait et une tarte, pour le monsieur, s'il vous plaît".

—Thank you very much Miss, I told her without taking my eyes off her, please let me know if you ordered something for yourself.

She responded that "No", that she was celebrating her sixtieth birthday with some friends. I said to her astonishingly:

—60 years old! My same age! But, you don't look your age.

—She gently told him that he didn't look his age either.

I immediately asked her if I could find an English speaking person to guide me and be able to communicate for me. She oriented me and told me to buy a book where I could find the most common translated words and then she said:

—Are you talking about a book in English but you spoke Spanish to me. Maybe you can find a book in Spanish and it would be easier for you.

I explained to her that no because I was American and my language was English and I commented that she looked latina. She answered that no, that she was French from a Spanish mother and French father, but that she had spent six years with her grandmother studying in Spain and that she had perfected the language. She continued talking:
—Well, I am going back to my table with my friends.

After showing her my gratitude I went back to the shop window and apparently the girl at the counter new what the word money was, I expressed myself with my hands that I was paying for the girls in that table, meaning her table.

Christopher stopped a few feet away from the entrance of the bakery to wait for her to leave the place. He could not believe that he would lose the sight of her beautiful eyes and those seductive lips. When he saw her leave, he approached her. She reacted very well because of his courtesy with all of them.
—Why did you do it?
—Simply because it is your birthday and you were very nice. I immediately added to my words:
—I don't want to lose contact with you, where can I contact you to take you out to dinner to a fine restaurant for your birthday. Then, I proceeded to introduce myself:
—My name is Christopher Smith, let me give my business card for my business in the United States and a card from the hotel where I am staying, you can call the hotel to confirm that I am registered there and that I have paid for the whole time of my stay in France. May I have your telephone number and where to locate you?

She was still distrustful and asked him:

—What are you looking for in me? Why so much interest...???

To that, I answered:

—Because you have been very nice to me and I feel as if I have known you all my life, please, give me the pleasure of taking you to dinner.

She kept staring at me for a few seconds and introduced her hand in her purse to get a business card and she gave it to me saying:

—You can contact me at this place, I own a Boutique a few blocks from here. Call me later and we will talk more, I have to go back to my business now.

He offered to accompany her but she said, "it is not necessary my business is just a few blocks from here". Christopher did not wait for her to call, when he got to the hotel he went straight to the front desk and asked the employee to get a very pretty flower arrangement for him to be delivered at her Boutique to Ms. Francesca Bardot. He pulled his business card and wrote on the back of it the following message:

I found out about a very good restaurant nearby and made reservations for both of us for tonight at 9:00 o'clock. Please don't leave me waiting. The restaurant's name is Le Maurice Alain Ducasse, 228 Rue De Rivoli. If you wish I can pick you up or we can meet at the restaurant. Call me and let me know. Thank you.

He took a second shower and sat to wait for the call that he never received. When it was close to 9:00 at night, he wore a tuxedo that he had brought with him and took a taxi to the restaurant. After waiting 15 minutes at the table he saw her coming into the restaurant. She was wearing an emerald green dress just like her eyes. It was all he saw from the distance. As she was approaching the table he started getting a little nervous. A date after so many years, made him feel like an adolescent. She was wearing high heels and her steps were not very firm. Christopher stood up as a courtesy sign when she got to the table and the waiter that accompanied her to the table accommodated the chair for her. Christopher wanted to act funny and friendly and greeted her in French:

—"Bonjour mademoiselle" —then she told him.

—But it is already night time, you have to say Bon Soir. He was happy because she accepted the invitation. The waiter was waiting for the orders and he asked for a bottle of Champaign, the best they had, if she liked it and he asked her to find out if the restaurant had "Blanc de Noirs" of limited edition. The waiter affirmed they did. Christopher wanted to know what was the the most popular dish and then she asked the waiter in french.

—"Quant a mes habitudes gastronomiques", the waiter responded in her language. "Vous pouvez varier enormement".

She told Chirstopher that there was a dish that included three different kind of fish with vegetables which was named "Le Jardin Marin", which is a very expensive dish.

—How expensive? Christopher asked the waiter.

—390 euros the waiter responded.

Then Christopher responded:

—Do you think that anything can be so expensive to celebrate the sixtieth birthday of a lady with Emerald Green eyes?

—How much would I have to pay for two Emeralds? And, notwithstanding the circumstances, I have them in front of me at no cost. The cost of this dinner is not important.

She was shy because of the compliment and generosity.

Then she honestly told him that she had never been in a restaurant of this nature adding:

—You have to be a wealthy person to afford these prices no matter how expensive the Emeralds can be.

The world stood still for both of them, she looked deep into his eyes and for several seconds both were speechless, then Francesca realized that the waiter was still standing in front of them waiting for the order with the napkin hanging from his arm and then she told the Waiter:

—I am sorry. We both want "Le Jardin Marin".

—The waiter took the order and left.

When they were alone again, she looked around the place astonished by the beauty of that restaurant: chandeliers hanging from the ceiling, the walls were covered by silk, pictures from other centuries, luxurious cups and dinnerware, the silverware appeared to be made of gold. How beautiful all of this is! It was a night to remember like if she was in a fairy tale with her blue prince in front of her. Many years had passed since she enjoyed a night like this. She was afraid to wake up. Her life was full of sad memories and a lot of work. She liked the gentleman a lot, because he was tall, very elegant, fair skin and his eyes were also of a light color. He was wearing a tuxedo that looked very good on him. She liked him from the first moment she saw him fighting like crazy over a coffee. Christopher, saw her thinking and asked her if there was something wrong with her.

—You are very distracted. Is it that you don't like my company?

Since she sinned of being sincere without any restriction she answered:

—All the contrary, I love your company.

—I was only contemplating the beauty of this place, I feel flattered with this birthday gift.

He expressed how happy her words made him and confirmed that his eyes had not lied to him when he saw the honesty and sensibility in Francesca.

—I have not met a woman such as you in many, many years. Don't think that this is a birthday gift for one night, You have me love struck. You are a witch; but don't worry I know that you are a good witch. I want this night to be the beginning of something beautiful between the two of us.

—But then she told him:

—Don't go so fast Christopher, you don't know me yet and you are already talking about something serious.

They ate very slowly, interacting and talking about their businesses, that was how she found out that he was the owner of a tire business and an investor in real estate, that he was a widower for over two years and had two children that would support him in everything. He also found out that Francesca was also self-employed and ran her business. She was the owner of the Boutique and the apartment where she lived, on the floor above her business, therefore, the small business consisting of two floors was hers.

Francesca also talked about her two daughters, Camille and Chloe, both lived in counties nearby because they never wanted to leave her alone, but they had their careers and their respective families. She has two grandchildren. Camille has a daughter named Sofia after Francesca's mother and Chloe has a son named Damien. She is a widow since she was 48 years old. Her husband was a fireman and had died in a fire. Since then she had never had a serious relationship. Sometimes she would date an old friend and go to have dinner with someone who was also lonely.

They left the restaurant and he asked if she wanted to take a taxi or have a walk through the streets of Paris to the Boutique. Francesca looked up to the sky and when she realized that the night was cool and beautiful, with a full moon and the sky full of stars she told him:

—Let's walk.

Two hours passed walking under the stars, talking about non-serious matters. Christopher got more and more excited. Listening to her voice his passions arose and when they finally got to her house he told her:

—I will pick you up tomorrow after work and will take you to a nice place. Francesca was a woman of a strong will but liked the man a lot, the champagne had gotten to her and the night was too beautiful and without even thinking too much, responded:

—Ok, pick me up tomorrow after work and let's go.

She had not finished the sentence when Christopher kissed her and she responded to his kiss. He couldn't believe what was happening and thought that she was probably drunk and that she would not want to go out with him the following day because he was very impertinent.

When Christopher arrived at the hotel, he was still inflamed with passion and so happy that when he saw the Bellboy he grabbed him by the hands and started dancing with him in a circle and then the Bellboy asked him.

—What is going on with you, Sir?

—I met a wonderful French woman.

Christopher headed to the elevator jumping and repeating, "wonderful, wonderful, wonderful" out loud. All the guests sitting in the lobby and by the front desk looked at him and commented that he was crazy. He laughed and asked the kid at the front desk to help him place a call to the United States where it was already day time. The maid answered the phone at his house and Christopher euphoric asked her:

—Please ask Richard to come to the phone?

—Hi, son.

—What's wrong dad?

—A lot is happening and nothing has happened he said.—Explain yourself dad. What's the issue?

—I have met a real princess. It seems like she has been made to perfection. She has the most beautiful green eyes in this world and she turned 60 years old today.

—What? A sixty year old princess? Please dad, call me again when you are sober.

—It's that you have never seen a woman as beautiful as her. I am very happy.

—Ok, dad. I am glad, I love you. Bye. Seems like he is losing it, Richard thought to himself.

CHAPTER V
JANUARY 19, 2006

Another beautiful morning in Paris. Francesca woke up in her apartment and could see through the open windows of her room that it was late compared to the time she usually woke up to go down to her Boutique and open its doors. Sometimes, at a very early time in the morning she had two or three customers waiting for her to open the doors of the shop "Imperial Boutique". She could not believe how many things had happened in such a short time.

Only 24 hours had passed since she met him at the coffee shop and they had a date, had dinner and kissed, she could not recognize herself. What spell had that man put on her that drove her crazy and made her behave in such an irrational manner? She tried to get up from bed and everything seemed to be going around. She was not used to drinking alcohol and apparently the best Champagne would make a higher effect than the cheapest. Then, she called the number of her Boutique and her loyal partner, employee and friend, Yanay, answered the telephone. She was a Spaniard, her parents brought her from Spain to help in the business. Yanay was an excellent dress maker even as Francesca was pretty demanding

—Hello my dear, it's good to know that you are already at the shop. I can't leave the bed and the customers should be arriving soon.

Her employee worried when she heard that and asked her:

—And, are you sick my dear?

—No. —said Francesca—. I have a hangover from the alcohol I had last night.

—You, with a hangover from alcohol?

—Yes.

—How come? You never drink.

—It's a long story Yanay. I will tell you later.

—Not that long, because a few hours ago you were sober.

—I told you I will tell you later. If Christopher calls, do not tell him that I feel bad, tell him that I have decided to sleep a little bit longer. Intrigued, Yanay asked:

—And who is Christopher?

—My blue prince.

—May I ask, in what castle you found him?

—Well, said Francesca, get on helping with the clientele. Bye.

—She went back to bed and she realized that Christopher knew nothing about her and she knew very little about him. He didn't even know that her Boutique also included a factory to make dresses of high class design. She studied dress designing in Cuba since this was her mother's job in Cuba and she helped her since he was only 10 years old. She was only 22 years old when she graduated as a dress designer in Paris.

Lying in bed she started a mental retroactive movie of her life. Not everything was a rose garden but she was very grateful to the Lord for being where she was. Incredible, but a long time had passed. When she was only six years old, her parents decided to send her to Spain with her maternal grandparents, because the economy in France was in decline. Her parents decided to move to America, namely Cuba, a young country where many Europeans would emigrate evading war and in search of a fortune. They didn't want to take the girl or the boy, with them until they had settled.

Three years had elapsed when the parents showed up to get the children and take them to Cuba. Her father was an administrator of a luxurious hotel in Havana, since he was fluent in English, French and Spanish and there were many American tourists in Cuba and he became the number one figure at the hotel. He had the same occupation in France.

They resided in an apartment in Havana in a very nice but not luxurious neighborhood. From this place you could see several hills and it was not that far from the hotel where her father worked. Also, there was a Catholic School directed by Mexican nuns for adolescents called "Maria Auxiliadora" because her parents believed that it was a place where she would feel good. At that school she took her First Communion and Confirmation. After that the nuns began to influence her life and the parents changed her for a very expensive good school, in which she studied until she was 14 years old when they had to go back to France.

In 1959 the President of Cuba administered over a dictatorship but suddenly left Cuba when a rebel movement took over. In the year 1960 the new government declared itself Communist. The business where her father worked was confiscated by the government and they had to go back to France. Her mother was used to a middle class form of life, and starting from zero again was very difficult for her. She suffered a nervous breakdown and it took a while to recover. Because of this issue Francesca had to study and run the house at the age 14. Her father started looking for work and found a job in the same chain of hotels, but her mother was not fit to have a job or perform the house chores, until she totally recovered and went back to be her old self.

Francesca was thinking that she got married too young, when she was only 18 years old. Studying until she was 22 and having her first daughter at 23. She was fully prepared to invest in her own business and bought her first Boutique also named Imperial Boutique. Five years after that, after looking for another child, she got pregnant again but lost the boy at birth. Years after that she conceived a baby girl. She did not want to have an only child as she didn't want the responsibility to fall on only one child's shoulders. Her first daughter was always of a strong character but the second daughter was quiet and sweet.

CHAPTER VI
A RELATIONSHIP

Christopher called the Boutique and Yanay answered the phone. He asked for Francesca. Yanay told him she wasn't there:

—Please, ask her to get in touch with me.

—She was curious and asked. Who are you?

—Christopher Smith.

—Are you interested in any merchandise from the store that I could help you with.

—No. Thank you.

When he finished the conversation, he took a taxi and visited the places of distribution of tires and looked at the way those businesses were functioning in that country, he was also wandering around the hotel and looking at houses and shops. He sat in a park for a while and looked at people walking their dogs. He also looked at the way the residents were dressed. He was thinking a lot about Francesca and what could be expected from the present and the future. Then after that looked for a telephone booth to call his children in the United States and find out how they were doing and let them know how he was. By the phone booth he felt the urge to call Francesca.

When Francesca answered the phone Christopher told her that he had called earlier. Then, she replied to him:

—I have called you twice and the receptionist at the hotel could not find you. I know you called me but I don't know why.

—First to look at your green eyes and secondly ask how you woke up.

—I woke up thinking that you don't lose time, you kissed me in less than 24 hours inadvertently.

—Didn't you like the kiss?

She did not respond and he was worried she would have had hung up on him and insisted.

—Are you there Francesca? You have answered because you really liked it, would you like to repeat that experience again? Yes or no?

She deviated the conversation and asked him:

—Besides the kiss and the green eyes what else do you want?

—I am on my way to pick you up, have lunch and go to a museum or place of interest and I need a translator with beautiful green eyes and a perfect figure.

—She immediately answered. That is easy, maybe at the front desk of the hotel you will find a translator with green eyes.

—What is wrong with you? Have I suggested anything that would bother you? Is that it?

Then more calmly he said:

—No, no, what I am saying is that I am waiting for a taxi to go and pick you up.

—I am telling you. I have to work and take care of my shop. You are on vacation but I am not, she replied:

"You have a life made far from me."

—Couldn't you leave your assistant taking care of the shop for a few hours ?

—I cannot push my responsibilities in others. This is my business and I need to supervise all that goes on here.

—I understand, but, if you were sick you would have to rely on your assistant and be absent for hours. I am on my way there, the taxi is here. And hung up.

—Hey, hey, what are you doing! Then, she began thinking out loud, this man is incredible, persistent and gets what he wants. Then, she screamed at Yanay, please hurry, I have to run and get dressed, my prince is picking me up. She then wore a white silk blouse and a tight black skirt to a length under the knee and wore a black beret in concordance with her attire. High heeled shoes and an Emerald Green scarf hanging over her shoulders. She painted her lips bright red. When she went downstairs, Yanay told her:

—This Prince is going to drive us bankrupt. Let me take a look at him and see how he looks.

Approximately 15 minutes later, a taxi stopped at the Boutique and he asked the taxi driver to stay that he wanted to hire him all day through midnight. He said: — don t worry I will pay you well. When he noticed that he was not understanding what he meant he tried making him understand with gestures, while he kept saying: "money no problem" Ok, ok! When Yanay saw him getting out of the car she called Francesca:

—Francesca, Francesca, your Prince Christopher is here, she said.

—I am not a prince, miss.

—Well, I don't know what you are, but, Francesca says you are her prince.

—You don't know how happy your words make me.

—You are also very pretty and young to be an experienced dress designer.

Francesca had gone upstairs to get her purse that she had forgotten in her apartment. When Christopher saw her he was hypnotized because by the way she was walking down. He was speechless and could only look at her and she noticed his stare and felt shy and told him. Are you going to say hello to me? And extended her hand at him but he took the hand in a way that he could kiss the hand, he had brought a rose in his suit and gave it to her, and told her:

—This rose is red like your lips. He rushed to open the door for her and said:

—Go on my queen, here is your prince because I just found out that I am a prince.

—Please, Christopher, where did you get that from?

—Your assistant just told me.

—How can that be! Yanay, you are crazy. You and I will talk over this when I get back. You are too gossipy.

—Then, it is true. You said it yourself.

He asked her to take him to a fast food place and she gave the taxi driver instructions to take them to "Café Du Monde", Christopher could not recognize the name of the place until they got there and she asked for a plate of the famous "Beignets, so he could try them. When Christopher realized those were the same doughnuts that he had in his honeymoon. He left a tip on top of the table, took Francesca's hand and insistently repeated:

—Let's go, let's go, let's get out of this place.

—Then Francesca asked him "What has happened to you? I didn't bring you to a bad place, on the contrary, it is a place known worldwide".

He answered to her:

—That is the problem that I know the place, because I went to a similar place in my honeymoon in New Orleans, with my deceased wife and it brought a lot of sad memories.

—I am sorry, it was not my intention to bring these remembrances that made you sad, if you want we can leave the date for another day.

—No. I would never in my life loose the opportunity to spend this afternoon with you, that is my past and it had a very sad ending, but you are present and my future. If so you wish.

She asked:

—Where are we going now?

—He suggested: Let's go to "McDonald's". I know there are McDonald's here and you are going to eat American food and an exquisite desert, an apple pie.

Then she said:

—You are so bossy Christopher! Could it be that I am the princess and you are the king?

But, he replied:

—Not dominant, no, I am only a man.

They ate a "Cheeseburger" with fries, coke and an apple pie and were talking nonsense and laughing for a long time.

When they left McDonald's she gave instructions to the taxi driver:

—The "Monsieur" wants to see a museum. I want you to take us to the best. The "Musee du Louvre". Then Francesca started taking to the taxi driver, "Les dimanches ma soer et moi, nous allions avec per au Musee du Louvre, mama resta a la maison, ell preparait un grand dejeuner pour toute la famille".

—Christopher said: What are you talking about? I don't want to be left out?

—Don't worry Christopher, we were talking about my father.

They arrived to the Museum and Christopher was astonished. It really is an impressive building out of comparison. She saw the way he looked at it and asked him.

—Do you like it? I hope it does not bring sad memories to you.

—No. It is an architectonic wonder. Before we go inside I would like to see the building all around. Do you know that the pyramids of crystal and iron that represent the entrance to the museum were designed by a Chinese-American architect? It is surprising that with so many French architects a Chinese-American had to design the museum. That proves that Americans are smart.

They were walking around the building and Christopher took her hand and she asked him:

—Why are you taking me by the hand?

—I don't want anybody picking on you, because there are some men that are looking at you.

She did not take her hand off from his and they kept walking around the building and continued being astonished by the museum itself and the works of art. They reached a place that was almost empty and Christopher started complaining and she turned towards him preoccupied:

—What happened to you?

—Seems like either sand or a bug got into my eye, can you blow it out?

She naively approximated her mouth to his eye to blow the eye and then he grabbed her by her neck and gave her a very long kiss, and pushed her against the wall of the building. Francesca pushed him by the chest and told him:

—What's wrong with you Christopher?

—It's that I suddenly went crazy, because when I look at you my blood boils, it is a love that gets into my bones and burns me inside and I lose my reasoning.

—Well, take it easy. We are not two adolescents, we are two grownups and there are people looking at us.

—I don't know about you, but I feel like an adolescent when I am with you. I feel as if I were fifteen years old, haven't you realized that I have found the half that I was missing, what I was looking for I found in you.

Then, she took his hands off her chest and took them

all the way to her neck and started kissing him warmly and softly:

—I never thought I would find my other half in an American.

They kept walking around the building very close to each other and holding hands. Now they didn't care about the rest of the world. They were living the life at 60.

They entered the museum and it was beautiful. Christopher said:

—I love the floor of the entrance. I feel like roller skating through all of it.

—The things that you American think about, you don't have an artistic mind, how can you think about roller skating at a place like this? Seems like kids stuff. Is it that you don't recognize all of the important art works in this place?

—Of course I know them: Elvis Presley, Frank Sinatra, The Beatles, Madonna, Michael Jackson. I can enumerate a lot more.

—Don't be dumb, I am referring to the painters, the sculptures and art works like the Mona Lisa by Leonardo DaVinci.

—Where is the art in this ugly woman? If it was your painting it would be worth looking at it, look how beautiful you look with that hat and the scarf? I am going to take a picture of you and put it up here. These poor people pay for looking at so many ugly faces.

—My love, behave yourself, we have paid for looking at art works not my pictures, please take your hands off my behind; you are making me feel uncomfortable. If you continue with this behavior, we are leaving!

—Then, why do you wear that little skirt so tight on your rear? Your butt is what attracts me, I am going crazy over it!

—Let me guide you and let's keep looking at the art works, that's what we came here for.

—Can't you tell that I am joking…? You take everything too seriously and it is not worth it. I know that there are paintings in this museum by Rafael, Botticelli, Tiziano, work by David and Delacroix and I am dying to see Medusa and the jewels of King Ramses II. Before getting here I used the computer at the hotel and I was looking into the most interesting sites at the museum. What happens is that you get so serious that I love looking at your face when I talk nonsense.

They spent most of the afternoon at the museum until it closed. Looked infinity at the works of art. When they left the museum Christopher told her:

—So sad that I left the mouse at the hotel.

—Do you have a mouse as a pet?

—No, I picked him up at a sewer to drop him by the side of a very refined lady.

—I am not going out with you anymore if you are going to behave crazy.

—Listen my love, this is very serious, how old are you? You told me you are sixty, so am I. That is not true we are twenty.

—How can we be 20 years old?

—The years that we have lived do not count, what counts is our love life, the sexual satisfaction, travel with the family, have time with them. We have a maximum of 20 years ahead of us with a good quality of life, do you understand now? Yesterday passed, tomorrow is not for sure, let's live today to the maximum.

—She replied: I am sorry I did not want to bother you, but, I cannot be like you, each person has his or her personality but, remember that opposites attract.

He started looking around and facing her and asked.

—Is there a "hot dog cart" around here? This has been a long walk without eating. I am dead hungry.

—We are in a luxurious museum, not a supermarket.

—I would rather go to a luxurious hotel and eat there and then I can show you my suite?

—No... What do you think? I am not anybody. You have already had several approaches today and I have not given you any response.

They asked the taxi driver to take them to a good Italian Restaurant, to have a good wine and eat some "Fetuccini Alfredo"?

—Do you like Italian food Francesca?

—If you behave like an adult. Yes, I do like it.

They ordered two cups of a good French Wine and two dishes to share, Fetuccini Alfredo and a Lasagna. When they finished eating they looked for a good burlesque theater show. When they were on their way to that place, he specified that he did not want an Opera or a Ballet, then they decided to go to the Burlesque. She complained because Christopher did not want to watch a fine performance but deep inside she found his craziness very funny.

It was a very pleasing night. He took her home and grabbed her by the hands when getting out of the taxi and told her:

—Let me go into your apartment so that I can use the restroom.

—No... I already know you...after you use the restroom you will not put on your pants. Use the bathroom at the Boutique. There is a restroom downstairs.

—No, thank you. I can wait until I get to the hotel.

—You are a bandit.

—Would you give me a kiss?

—Yes, but under certain conditions. Put your hands on my shoulders. Five inches away...hands on top. You have already touched enough today.

—That is not fair, a kiss like that tastes the same as an egg without salt. Totally tasteless.

—Oh... without salt or nothing, you choose!

—Under those conditions let me put my hands on your shoulders.

Instead of that, he grabbed her by the neck and put his chest close to her breasts.

—Leave me alone, the taxi driver who is a young man is looking at us, and is going to think that we are crazy.

—See you tomorrow. I will pick you up early at 9:00 to have breakfast, my beautiful French girl.

When she put her head on the pillow everything was turning around, but not because she was drunk. It was dizziness out of desire, because she felt the same as him. And she was thinking – sleeping with a man you like and that attracts you and make love all night is a temptation, but, I don't want to suffer because of a man after so many years, a man who I might not even see again. That is my fear. But, he is an attractive man, vigorous, wealthy, good looking, very funny and very crazy. I don't laugh, but I love his craziness. I have gone through too many years of being formal I feel that life should give me the opportunity to feel like a woman, because like he said, I only have 20 years or less to live. Little by little she fell asleep dreaming about the same things she was thinking and hoping those things would become true, but she had never been too optimistic. Around 1:00 a.m. the phone rang. She jumped out of bed and was nervous when she answered the phone.

—Who is it, who is it?

—It's me Francesca, Christopher.

—What are you doing calling at this hour? You made me nervous.

—I just wanted to ask you if you have also fallen in love with me, I can't go to sleep with that doubt.

—Do you know something Christopher? You are going to sleep without knowing that! See you tomorrow… and hung up on him.

CHAPTER VII
BEGINNING OF OUTTINGS AND MUTUAL FEELINGS

Yanay was fixing the windows of the store to show the new summer collection, when she saw a taxi approaching the shop. It was 9:00 a.m.

—Is it possible that this prince is already here?

Grumbled Yanay. Right at that moment she felt a noise of heels down the stairs, she turned and told Francesca:

—Where are you going at this time? Is your prince going to pay me double for doing my work and yours?

—Don't worry Yanay, when he goes back to the United States you can take a vacation.

He touched the bell and Yanay not very happy with the circumstances looked at him very serious, Francesca moved Yanay and she personally opened the door for him. When Christopher saw her he asked her:

—Where are you going Francesca? We are going to walk all day. We are going to the Eiffel Tower in the morning and the Versailles Castle in the afternoon. I want to visit the center of the city to buy you a pretty gift, please change your high heel shoes and wear a more comfortable attire, look at me, I am wearing a pullover and a jean. She responded:

—Why didn't you tell me?

—If it is too much for you to change clothes, I can help.

—Really? How funny you are! You take whatever excuse to reach your objective.

When Yanay and Christopher were alone, she told him:

—You are a little fresh. How can you state that you are going up with her to change her clothes. It is certain that you know nothing about her, she is a very decent woman.

She has to be very much in love with you to go out in such a rush. Let me tell you, she has had a lot of men after her and she had never accepted an invitation before.

Yanay nodded her head from one side to the other and was saying:

—I cannot believe it. Then, Christoper replied:

—Ah…! I forgot something in the car.

When he came back he had brought two bouquets of roses. One bouquet red and the other pink and then he told Yanay:

—The pink roses are for you, because you are a wonderful girl. Please put the red roses in a vase for Francesca. If not, we will never leave this place.

—Thank you very much. You are a gentleman. Francesca was already getting to the first floor and he told her.

—How happy I am. Yanay answered the question that I asked you last night and you didn't want to answer.

—What question did Yanay answer?

—She told me that you are very much in love with me.

Francesca was spewing flames through her eyes when she turned to look at Yanay.

—What are you doing? When did I tell you that I am in love with him?

—It is not necessary, you can tell just by looking at you, said Yanay.

Then, Christopher asked her:

—Well, is it true or not what Yanay said? Francesca looked at him and responded:

—I don't know if my declaration is going to be my sentence, but, I think I am in love with a guy that is picking up mice in the street.

Yanay jumped and asked if it was true that he picked up mice. He responded to Yanay:

—Do you want a pet?

—Don't you even try.

Francesca told him that he had been playing that game since the night before, but, that the mouse was a lie. Christopher was planning on going with her to get her promise gift. They left in the taxi, went to have breakfast. When the taxi left them at the coffee shop they asked the taxi driver to come back in three hours and to pick them up in the same place.

—The breakfast seemed like the breakfasts they had in Cuba when they were kids, "café con leche" with toasts and expresso at the end.

He had already asked where to find a jewelry store at the Hotel. He took her to the store by the hand. They stood in front of the window of a Jewelry Store and asked Francesca:

—What do you like from this window?

—I don't have anything in mind, what is this a proposal? Said Francesca.

—Yes, a proposal. I propose that we walk a long way together. What do you think about my proposal?

She pointed out to a pearl necklace with the closure of an emerald, because she did not expect the necklace to be that expensive. The jeweler called the owner and told him that those customers wanted to buy that necklace, then, the owner asked Christopher if he was aware of the cost of that jewel. When she knew the price she turned to him and told him that she had just confirmed that he was crazy. But he calmed her down letting her know that she didn't have to worry about the price.

—I am not going to allow you to buy me such an expensive gift, said Francesca.

—Expensive? I don't know about works of art, but I know

about jewels and this one is priced right. What I wouldn't pay to look into the Emeralds of your eyes!

Then, he pulled his black card out of his wallet. The store asked for an identification and he showed them his passport. They tried the card to make sure that he had enough credit. Also called the International Bank to make sure that the card had not been stolen or was lost. Christopher asked for the delivery of the necklace to the address she was going to give them. Francesca called Yanay from the jewelry store and asked her to put the delivery in the safe deposit box immediately upon arrival.

They went walking and looking at the windows of the shop and after that they went to the Eiffel Tower and bought tickets to go up the tower. When entering the tower, he commented that besides the point that France took all the merit for the construction of the tower and gave the credit to Gustave Eiffel for the design of the tower, which is considered a French Monument, the person in charge of the construction of the tower was a Cuban named Guillermo Perez Dressler, but that this is practically unknown. Francesca made a sudden turn, very upset and told him:

—I am not going to believe that. It had to be a Cuban and not a French. How can you think that I am going to believe that?

—If you don't believe me research it, when you get to your place. If it is not true you can call me whatever you'd like, but, if it is true you have to kiss me twelve times in public.

She called Yanay over the phone and told her:

—Look for this information in the computer and call me back.

They continued going up by the elevator and when they reached the top of the tower, they could see most of Paris. What a beautiful sight. You can see all cardinal points from up here. The position in which it was erected was also wonderful. Christopher was leaning by the back against the fence and then, he told her:

—Apparently the pearl necklace has influenced a lot and you are more receptive, I never thought that you would lean on me at the top of the tower in front of everybody. If I had thought about it, I would have bought you a diamond necklace from the beginning.

—What is this all about? What do you think about me? That you can buy me with a necklace?

—I only think that you are wonderful.

At that moment her cell rang, it was Yanay. She told Francesca that it was true, that it was a Cuban who constructed the Eiffel Tower. She said thanks, Yanay, turned towards Christopher and started kissing him all through the face and the mouth. He had forgotten about what he had said of the construction of the tower.

—What is this? Is this also because of the necklace?

—Don't be so conceited, I lost the bet.

—Ah…! Then the crazy American was right?

—You are always right, but, remember that famous saying, "women never lose but when they don't win they get even". A French man whose last name was Eiffel also contributed to the construction of the tower.

—I never said anything to the contrary, but the Cuban was the contractor.

They left walking out of the structure towards the taxi, this structure was also called the "Dame of Iron". Then, Christopher started feeling sick, he felt nauseous and felt very bad. His stomach was making noises and felt like vomiting. When they were approaching the car he had to throw up in the middle of the street. He asked the driver to take him as soon as possible to the hotel. She insisted in taking him to a hospital but he did not feel like going. When he got to the hotel he spoke to the man at the front desk and asked him to call a doctor for him as soon as possible. Christopher asked Francesca to leave in the taxi and go home but she insisted in staying until he felt better. When they were at his bedroom he had to run to the restroom because he kept throwing up. Then she grabbed the phone and asked to get a doctor urgently or to call an ambulance.

When the doctor arrived he checked Christopher very thoroughly while he kept vomiting. The doctor asked him what it was that he ate, then she explained that he had coffee and milk with toasts and a glass of water. The doctor said that it probably was a bacteria because he had been drinking water that was contaminated. The doctor said that he was going to give him a shot to stop the vomiting.

He fell asleep and woke up several hours later. Looking throughout the room he found Francesca in a chaise lounge completely dressed and looking as if she was cold. He was in his underwear, somebody had undressed him while being asleep. He went to the bathroom and totally washed himself, put on some perfume and changed his underwear, he didn't want her to see him so messy. Then, once clean, he got near her and gave her a kiss, and told her:

—Francesca, wake up and come and lie in the bed so that you can be more comfortable, I don't feel well but you cannot continue lying down in that position. It is too late for you to take a taxi. I rather have you stay lying down besides me. I will not bother you. As I previously told you I don't feel well, get comfortable and rest.

—I want you to ask for something simple for me to eat right here.

—I will ask for a Canada-Dry, said Christopher.

She wanted a juice and a toast with cheese. He called the room service and in a few minutes they had the delivery. After that, Francesca, undressed and only kept her brass and panty on, under the bed sheet and he behaved like a gentleman to do what he had promised, besides that he was not fit to do anything else. They slept until 8:00 a.m. and then she got dressed and left for her business.

When she got to her business Yanay was waiting for her pretty worried.

—Where did you spend the night? With your prince?

—Yes I spent all night with my prince, but, he was not with me, something he ate made him sick, he got real sick and I spent the whole night taking care of him.

—What a nasty honeymoon! Said Yanay.

Francesca asked Yanay to show her the delivery brought by the jewelry store. When she opened the package, Yanay looked very surprised and asked if it was faux or legitimate. Then she answered that, it's worth more or less all of the merchandise in our complete Boutique. Yanay continued asking:

—What are you going to do? When are you going to wear it?

—I don't know, let's see if we can go to a Fancy Theater or The Opera, but that is going to be difficult, because I don't want to take Christopher to see something he doesn't like.

Yanay suggested something unexpected:

—Why don't you wear it and lie down in the bed completely nude?

—I don't want that jewel to opaque my body.

—When are you going to be his?

—If you only knew that I was thinking about that all night,

it is time already, I am not a young girl and he seems to be a serious man and really into me. There is time for everything and I am not going to be his so soon because he is going to think that I am an easy woman and you know that I have not been with anybody else. He has talked about his life and marriage a lot and about his wife and has told me that he was very much in love with her and that he takes her flowers every week and a dish with her favorite desert. Then, Francesca told Yanay that she had already asked him why had he gets her a desert if she cannot eat and he gave me a smart answer:

—Why do you put flowers for your deceased husband if he cannot see them nor can he smell them?

—I had no other alternative but to admit it. He is a family man and a business man. He is very playful and he looks like a young crazy American, but that is what I like the most from him. Then Yanay asked her:

—How is it that as serious as you are have fallen in love with a young crazy American?

—Remember that cold and hot waters, when mixed up become warm and it is enthusiastic, that is why. Let me add something to this, before I finish, I am not interested in his position, I am interested in his love and respect and he has demonstrated to be a gentleman, besides being a little crazy. What I fear the most is that if we get into a serious relationship, he could ask me to leave and go live with him in the United States, since he will not abandon his life, but I also have mine here, my children and my business. That worries me a lot. That is my fear, that is why I have resisted.

—Then, I am no one in your life? said Yanay. Are you leaving me behind?

—I will not leave you behind either, but you already have

your own family and I know, you will not want to leave your family behind. You think that I have not noticed that there is a policeman picking you up every afternoon?

At that moment the phone rang and Francesca ran to the phone and answered. It was Christopher that was not feeling well.

—Hello my Queen. How are you? Then, he continued…

—What are you doing this afternoon? I am feeling weak and would appreciate it if you could spend the afternoon here with me. I need that a lot.

—Don't worry, I am heading over in a little while. Yanay, indiscreet, as usual, said:

—Who called you, your prince or your little crazy American? How do you want me to call him?

—I choose my little crazy American.

—How do you want me to call yours? Policeman or Gendarme?

—I prefer you to call him gendarme, he is the guy that makes me happy.

CHAPTER VIII
BEGINNING OF AN INTENSE ROMANCE

As soon as Christopher hung up the phone, he called the front desk and asked for two bottles of champagne, a bunch of pink roses, a big tablecloth. Also asked for a jar of ice for the champagne and a bowl of strawberries dipped in chocolate, a dish with a variety of cheeses and caviar, as soon as possible.

Francesca took a shower, dressed in comfortable but refined attire because she was going to a luxurious hotel, but, since she was thinking about taking care of a sick person she had to wear comfortable clothes. When she was leaving her shop Yanay screamed at her:

—Did you shower? Remember that you are heading to the wolf's cave and if you go like "Little Red Riding Hood". The wolf might eat you.

—Oh, Yanay, please? He is sick.

—Keep on thinking that way, I wouldn't be so sure.
Said Yanay.

—You know something. Whatever has to happen happens.

—That's the way to talk!

Then, Francesca took a taxi and left for the hotel. In the meantime, he had already taken a shower and was waiting for her with a plush robe very tight in the waste without any underwear. At that moment he received a call from the reception of the hotel and announced that a lady named Francesca was asking to go to his room. He gave orders for her to go upstairs and he waited for her by the door and they gave each other a kiss.

—How do you feel Christopher? You don't look that bad.

She thought that Yanay was right, she was in the "wolf 's lair". What neither the wolf nor Yanay knew is that she had brought the necklace in her purse and that she would wear it at the precise moment.

In the bedroom there was a French tune that Julio Iglesias was singing, the name of the son in French "La vie en Rose" (which means the life in roses). She immediately recognized the song.

—Do you know that song? Christopher asked.

—Of course, it is the Life in Rose.

—That is my life when I am with you, a rose garden, Francesca also observed that there were a bunch of pink roses, a bottle of champagne, strawberries deepened in chocolate, caviar and cheese. It was all disguised by a transparent curtain. I am very nervous she thought but I am going to put the necklace on.

—Ah! I see you blushing. Do you want me to call the reception and ask for a thermometer in case you have fever.

—No, no. It is a fever of passion when I look at you.

—I believe that you invented a sad story to make me come here, but, there is nothing aching in your body, you are a little crazy. He responded to her as follows:

—May I dance with you and sing in your ear some lyrics of a song by Luis Miguel? Do you know who I am talking about?

—Of course, he is an internationally known singer and you being American, how do you know music in Spanish?

—I do because my kid's maid is Mexican and she is always listening to Spanish music in the radio.

They began dancing and he was singing "Underneath the Table" in a low voice into her ear. The song goes like this:

"I am dying to take you to my hideout and it is that you don't know what you make me feel. If you could get into me for a minute you would know how my blood melts, that kills my pride, I would like to have you in my arms and it

is because I cannot be without you for a minute, in this space, that is now yours".

She replied:

—That song is beautiful.

Then his lips softly started touching her ear and neck. Then his hands started moving through her back all the way to her waist.

—What can I do with this reception? What do you want?

—I want you to be mine!

He continued touching her breasts under the opened bra while they kept dancing to the romantic music of Julio Iglesias. She left her chin on top of his shoulder, then, he took the liberty of taking her blouse and bra off leaving her breasts uncovered. He was astonished looking at those perfect breasts without surgery at her age. She softly moved her hand to his chest and with the other hand opened the belt of his robe. Inadvertently, touched the man's most distinctive organ, it surprised her. She didn't know where to hide. She told him:

—I did not expect this, specially being sick. I now realize how sick you were last night, I slept with you only with my underwear on, and you didn't notice it.

—Yes, but then I kept thinking all day, how possibly I could have missed that opportunity, because of the shot I got for vomiting and that took me to this moment. You will not reject me now, right?

—No, I am all yours.

He took her skirt off and let it go down the legs to the floor, immediately taking her panties off and also let it go down the legs to the floor. He commenced to caress her rear, he threw her clothes onto the floor and he turned her back against him, then, he softly moved his fingers around her vagina. At that moment, she was feverish and ready to ask for a thermometer.

—I am like a dormant volcano that this man has awaken, that erupts and provokes an undetermined passion in me.

—What happens to my little French girl that her eyes are so wide?

—It's that I am having an exceptional feeling passing through my skin, my body is trembling and I am having goose bumps of pleasure. I don't know what you have done with me to take me to this ecstasy. I am all yours, please take me to the bed.

When she got to the bed it was covered by a nylon table cloth. He told her:

—Lie down and put this pillow on your head. Trust me. I want you to feel all mine. Then, he took a bottle of champagne from behind the curtain and opened it. Walked towards her without a cup and when he approached her he started pouring drops of the champagne all over her body, from her neck to her feet, she jumped and told him:

—What is this? Are you fixing me to eat me later?

—Wait, I have not finished.

—What are you going to do to me now?, little crazy.

—Don't worry, I will bring the rest now.

He went and took the bunch of pink roses and started putting the petals all over her body, then he took a rose and put in on top of her pelvis.

—What are you doing?

—A garden on your body, I want to move my lips all throughout your skin and take the petals off with my lips.

She was not talking, she was only whipping and kept saying Oh, oh, oh, not because of pain but pleasure.

—I have never imagined living a fantasy like this, you took me to the sky.

—That is precisely what I wanted, that you would feel for

me what you never felt for another man.

When she was out of the transit of passion turned to him and kissed all of his body. But that was not the end of it, Francesca told him she was going to take a shower to rest for a little while. While she was taking the shower he picked the bed up and opened the cold bottle of champagne and prepared the snacks.

After taking a shower, she combed her hair, made up a little bit and took the necklace out of her purse and put it on leaving the bathroom totally naked. She was only wearing the necklace. He was astonished when he saw her, so beautiful, she looked like a naked fairy. She noticed his reaction and his look. He then said some inaudible words and kept repeating:

—Oh, oh, oh...! My God. I was not expecting this, he took her in his hands and took her back to the bed and wrapped her in silky sheets. At that moment they started dancing the eldest erotic dance of all times.

—I am now living Cinderella's story in my Prince's Arms for real. I am living this not in a story but in real life. I feel very happy!

When he saw the honesty in her words, besides how simple and blunt she was expressing herself, Christopher's eyes watered, she noticed it and full of the deepest emotions she got emotional too and told him:

—You have wet me with champagne covered me with rose petals, carry me to a bed of silk sheets and have filled me with food fit for a Princess. I cannot call you my little crazy guy, you are a complete gentleman and I am honored with your love. You are wonderful!

They started drinking champagne and eating, they sat on a bench in the balcony and were enjoying the beautiful sight of the city. The night was falling and they could see the beauty of Paris. They were both dressed in Plush Robes from the hotel and kept drinking champagne. He felt happy again and she felt drunk because of the alcohol. They were playing and dancing in the balcony. When they entered the room, she took her robe off and kept saying:

—My prince, come back and bathe me again with champagne. Cover my body with rose petals and eat me.

—I am ready to eat you!

Francesca had regained her sexual appetite and was acting crazy under the influence of the champagne and all of a sudden she fell asleep on the rug. Then, he took her to bed in his arms, he took the necklace off her neck and put it on her purse. A little while after that he went to lie in bed with her and fell asleep again. Around 4:00 a.m., she started pouring drops of water on his face and kept telling him:

—Christopher wake up, the night is long.

Christopher woke up scared because he was totally asleep and thought she was hallucinating because of the effects of the alcohol.

—Are you drunk my dear?

—No. I am very much awake, what happens is that you have opened Pandora's Box and now, beware because it is me who will constantly attack you.

He asked himself, WOW! What have I done? Francesca without being invited into bed, threw herself on top of him and began making love to him. It was a battle of love until the end. She got up and took a shower and then when he looked at the time, he told her:

—My dear, get dressed, we are taking a trip in Paris' rapid train.

She sat in front of him very serious and told him:

—We are going to have a serious talk now. What is your

next step?

—Meet your children because I want them to know that I am very firm in my proposition and I want you to be my wife in the future.

—You know that we have a conflict because you reside in the United States and your business and your family are there and I have all of that here. I know you will not resign to your interests and it would very difficult for me to abandon all that I have achieved by myself.

— I don't want to be selfish. Your business is very attractive and has a lot of history in your life. It has been of support to you and your family, but, mine is more productive because it is a big business and it is more solvent and we can be together. I promise you a comfortable life and without worries with me.

—Then, what do I do with my daughters and my business? She asked.

—We can sell your business or give it to your children or to Yanay. I can remunerate you for the value of your business and just give it to them. I cannot resign to my children either, I wished you could spend some time with me over there and then we can legalize your status for a marriage of a life time because once you enter my country married to an American Citizen and an investor all will be easier in the United States. As soon as you are an American Citizen you can claim your daughters and in between, your daughters can visit us and we can visit them. Remember the Bible is very clear about that, where it is established that the wife will leave her parents and will form her new family and will follow her husband.

Christopher continued:

—We are not thinking of leaving anybody behind, remember that love is also sacrifice and through that sacrifice you receive a big benefit at the end, that is what I propose: "love each other until death do us apart". And, if you wish, we will form a family.

She got dressed and after thinking for a while, told him that she could not respond immediately, then she asked him to give her some time.

—Very good, I agree. Have that margin of time, just think that we have very little time left in this trip. We are of age and we cannot wait years to make a decision. This reflection I will tell you now is very real, think about it because death is so certain that has all the patience to wait for us.

—Christopher, listen, let's make this decision when we meet again, we only have four days left to be together. If you don't come back, how do you think I am going to feel? I don't even want to think about it. Maybe you won't believe me, but, I have had other men after me. Many men have insisted for a long time and I didn't sleep with any of them. Besides that, I gave myself to you with a passion unknown to me. I never thought to live this romance at my age. I have never given so many kisses and caress like I have done with you. Please, let's talk when you come back to France or when I go to your country. Now, please take me home so that I can change and spend another unforgettable day with you.

—Please hurry or we are going to miss the rapid train. Just like that rapid train we can miss life, waiting for a meeting that I desire, but, it might never come.

—Don't talk to me like that. Are you sick? Or, is it that I have just been someone that passed by your life.

—I am sorry to talk about material things, as a proof of this crazy love that I feel for you. I can be an American millionaire but, I have been brought up by a family of principles and before entering into your life I had formed a reputable family, but, going back to the material things, do you think that a necklace like I gave you is for someone that just passed by your life? No my French Beauty. I cannot conceive having a day where I cannot get lost in the flame of your eyes and I never thought I would find love at 60 years of age.

They took a taxi and went to Francesca's business that was not far from the hotel. That is the reason why they met in that coffee shop that was located near both places. When they got to the Boutique, Francesca ran up the stairs and changed cloth from the day before and chose a pant suit of a very light texture. A design very classy, brown and wore low heel shoes, she retouched her make up and put some perfume on. She left the bedroom in a rush but then realized that she had not taken her purse.

Christopher told her:

—You are always forgetting your purse, you have to be careful in the streets, why don't you leave the purse here and take only the phone and the keys in a smaller purse.

—Christopher, you are right, but then I cannot retouch my lips.

—Why so much retouching if I like you without makeup and naked? Let me tell you that you look beautiful.

She took a piece of paper and a pen to left Yanay a message. "Good morning my friend, I am leaving with my King to spend another dreamy day. Kisses, Francesca". When Yanay got to the boutique an hour later and read the note, told herself: Look at that, the French Lady is in love.

CHAPTER IX
TRIP TO NIZA

They arrived to the rapid train station in Paris and bought two tickets to Nice. The trip would take approximately five and a half hours. It was early, 7:15 in the morning. The train was leaving at 7: 30 and would arrive to Nice at 12:30. Christopher bought first class tickets with a cabin.

—Why cabin?

—To make love at the same movement of the train. I have never made love in a train or a plane.

—Do you feel more of a man in a train or a plane or in a car?

—That is only a fantasy, in the car I have experimented it, and you?

—No, I am not a show off.

—Oh yes. Who is going to believe that with those eyes and that movement in bed? You are like a "Spanish tale about a cat called Maria Ramos that throws a rock and hides the hand".

—How sad, you didn't tell me that when we were at my house. I would have brought a sensuous night gown to move my hips even more.

—You don't need a sensuous night gown I liked you naked and with the movement of the train, you won't even have to move.

Francesca started kissing him in front of the ticket cabin and told him:

—I like you so much. I don't know what you have done to me that I have lost my senses.

—I can see that you have lost your way! Kissing me in front of all these people and don't even realize what you are doing! He continued...

—I touched your behind in the museum and you got mad, you called my attention back then and now I have to call your attention because of your behavior.

—That was before the champagne, the rose petals, the strawberries and some other things that I have to tell you in a low voice in the cabin when we are alone. Said Francesca.

—I have already told you that I am afraid of you, but we have more than five hours in the cabin.

—It is nice to know that the movement of the train will help me because five hours in the cabin with you, will leave me so tired that I won't be able to look around in Nice, said Christopher.

—Is it possible that we will not be able to look at the countryside at some point?

—I only need the landscaping of your naked body and your green eyes illuminating the two mountains that you have in your chest, like Mount Everest and the river that goes through your body. I don't need a better scenery than that. But I want to see Nice and meet your younger daughter, Chloe, and her family.

—But, she is not expecting us, they are working.

—Please call her and let her know that we are in a train going to her place, that we should be arriving around noon and will spend a few hours with them. We have to take the train back at 7:00 tonight, that means that we will only be with them until 6:00.

There was a sign in French, English and Spanish stating that the train station in Nice had access to many ways of travelling to the passengers' destination, same as the airport.

—Nice is a city easy to walk around.

—Are you crazy Christopher? You have no idea as to the

distances that you have to walk.

When they got to the cabin and were "discovering the river that goes through Mount Everest," Francesca's cell rang. It was her daughter responding to her call. Very surprised and happy, she told her mother that she would pick them up with her husband. It was a few minutes interruption but anyhow it was nice to know that they were being picked up.

After that interruption they went back to their discoveries when Francesca advised him that they had already been two hours in the cabin and that she had not seen the countryside at all. Then, he asked her not to worry that two hours in the sky they could easily come back to earth and watch the countryside.

—Yes. I know, said Francesca. On the way back to Paris we will go back to the sky and then we can go to sleep in the cabin. Everything cannot be a love fantasy.

—Well, enjoy the fantasy while you can, because there are moments in which circumstances do not permit to enjoy a fantasy.

They got to Nice and her daughter introduced Christopher to her husband, neither of them spoke English or Spanish, but Francesca served as an interpreter.

The couple invited them to a restaurant, but, since they had already had lunch at the train and had paid for a fancy dinner on the cabin in the evening, they declined the invitation. Then Chloe asked her husband to stop at a deluxe bakery to get some snacks consisting of coffee, sweets and "tout an assortment de biscuits" (French for a variety of pastries).

When the daughter, the son-in-law and the mother started a conversation, Christopher separated from them and went to play with the kid, which was three years old, because he noticed that they were talking about a problem, because of the expression of their eyes and the way they moved their mouth. You could tell that there was tension in the conversation. He had no idea as to what was going on but Francesca looked at him while talking to them and he could see sadness in her looks and the illumination irradiated by her eyes was gone.

The boy kept pulling him from his pants and kept telling him things that he couldn't understand, but, he threw himself on the floor with the kid to play with small metal cars and notwithstanding the importance of the conversation at times Chloe would look at Christopher and smiled at him. She was very pretty and resembled her mother a lot.

A little while later they put on a cowboy American movie on TV translated to French. It was a movie that he had already seen played by Clint Eastwood "Ten Unforgiving", since it was a good movie that was awarded several "Oscars" and was considered a classic in its kind, he started watching it and enjoyed the movie which brought memories of his youth. The family also enjoyed watching the movie with Christopher, besides the fact that they had to read the subtitles in French.

They drank wine, ate cheese and exquisite French Pastries of different kind. Chloe asked her mother to let Christopher know that they were very happy to meet him, that they had certain opinion about Americans, who are considered to be cold persons but after meeting him, they totally changed their opinion. Then he asked Francesca to let them know that because of the intervention of the American Soldiers that sacrificed their lives in Normandy in the Second World War, their children didn't have to speak German and were able to have a flag of their own. She interpreted for them and they did not respond a single word to that. Christopher immediately told them. What happens? You don't have to be so serious about this. It is only my opinion and I feel good to know that you like me.

Francesca translated again what he said. They laughed and it was 6:00 o'clock already and they were taken to the train station. Like always when there is a separation, both the mother and daughter cried a little. Chloe gave Christopher a kiss and in her poor English she said:

—Listen, please take good care of my mother and make her happy. She deserves being happy.

Chloe's husband in form of a joke said:

— "Bye Father-in-law" and also gave a strong shake of hands.

Christopher was speechless with such a nice welcome and goodbye. They were friendly and warm and he could only say:

—Thank you very much. Whenever you want to visit the United States you can come to my house where you will be very welcomed. These are not merely words. It's an invitation to Francesca's wedding. She immediately responded:

—You were called father-in-law, you have invited them to our wedding and I have to remind you that I have not accepted yet.

—Oh yes, you'll see! Then he went down to his knees and looking a Chloe he said:

—I am officially asking you permission to marry your mother.

—I have already given it to you.

He was delighted with Chloe, she was very pretty, sweet and honest girl. It was worth taking the rapid train to meet her and pay the high cost of the tickets. Francesca commented:

—You are so quiet Christopher.

—I am a sentimental person just like you.

He hugged her and gave her a kiss in the mouth when entering the train. He carried her to get into the train.

—What are you doing my love?

—I am carrying the future Mrs. Smith to the train of dreams.

When they got to the train it was almost dinner time, Christopher was dying to eat a hot meal and he was served an exquisite lobster soup and crepes (very thin unsweetened pancakes), filled with asparagus and melted cheese. French bread with butter and a cup of white wine.

After that he was served some sort of American coffee that tasted like heaven and a desert very similar to a Cuban Desert. His mind flew to the City where he lived in Cuba, the Province of Matanzas, the city where he grew up and made it difficult for him to get used to the American ways, being a native American. Even his parents were missing the Cuban cuisine when the family gathered in the table for a special occasion and were served American meals, the tears would run down their faces.

The day after one of those occasions and conversations when we were coming back from the business, my mother surprised us with a Cuban Meal consisting of black beans, white rice, fried pork bits and a lettuce and tomato salad. Christopher felt like if it was Christmas Eve in Cuba and his smaller sister Christy, asked her mother:

—This is what you have to cook every day, no more turkey or broccoli, that's it, we were brought up in Cuba.

The father laughing said:

—We have a couple of Cubans here and we didn't know,

then he told the kids:

—Don't worry when Cuba becomes a free country we will go back.

Christopher was thinking that those days were beautiful days no matter how hard they were. I had my parents with me, which I don't have now. I only have my kids and this French Girl that God has brought into my life at the precise time.

They finished dinner and went back to the cabin to rest, but he saw Francesca no matter how she tried to hide it, she was worried and sad, she was looking by the window of the train but her eyes were getting red, she did not have a definite expression and it looked like her thoughts were far away. It seemed like she was crying in silence. Then he asked her:

—What is wrong, Francesca? Do you want to look at the countryside or do you want to have a conversation with me? Listen to me, by the experience acquired in my life I have learned that the life is made of stages, if you are going through a difficult stage, remember that it is only that "a stage", temporary and it will all change, but don't let it pass without learning from it. Every problem brings a lesson.

—You are so eloquent and your words are beautiful!

—I don't deserve that credit. I read it in a book. I suggest that you lie down for a while and try to rest, because tomorrow is another day.

They started caressing and she told him talking near his ear in a low voice:

—I love you, Christopher. I don't know why I feel like if I have known you all my life, you are a good man, a gentleman and a man of a very simple heart, besides being successful and a business man, you have chosen me being a simple dress maker. Like I have told you before this is like Cinderella's story and I am afraid to lose my shoe at midnight.

—No my love, you are not losing only your shoe, you are going to lose it all, the shoes, the dress, the panty... everything and I am ready to attack by all fronts.

—Come here my love, you can only think about attacks. Or is it that the lobster soup was an aphrodisiac for you? Have you forgotten that I also had the lobster soup?

He spoke very mellow and said:

—This is getting good: start fighting, whoever loses shows the white flag for peace.

—I know, I already know your tactics, hum... and they spent some time enjoying each other, after that they fell asleep until they got to Paris. When getting off the train, she asked him to take her to her apartment and he said no.

—You are my official fiancée and you are going to my bed.

—No, no, no, I know what you are capable of and I am too tired to be bathed in champagne.

—No, Francesca. We are going to take a shower and lie down and talk, I know you are worried about your daughter, you haven't told me but I kept hearing "Camille" in all of your conversations, when we arrived and they mentioned her, your face totally changed, I am not indiscreet but I want to know if I can help you and try to dissipate that worry or pain.

She then said: I can't not hold this in anymore, started crying and told him what was going on all the way to the hotel. She explained that her daughter's husband after twelve years of marriage told her daughter that he was leaving the house. Abandoning her and their daughter who is only 10 years old. My daughter started investigating and found out that he is dating a much younger woman.

—Please Francesca, we have to ask for a meeting with both of them, as soon as possible. Ask her if tomorrow for lunch or early hours in the afternoon we can go and visit them, then I will have the opportunity to meet your daughter and your granddaughter. You might doubt it, but I am a pretty good preacher and maybe I can help at this time. Everything is possible if you want to. Tomorrow the sun will be out for everybody.

When they got to the hotel he asked for a pill for headache and also ordered a small sandwich and a soda. They fell asleep almost immediately, it seemed like the trip in train drained them.

The following morning, they had breakfast at the restaurant in the hotel. They also went shopping inside the hotel because Christopher wanted to take a little token to Camille and to the girl. He saw Cuban cigars and bought them for Francesca's son-in-law, he would have never thought that he would find those cigars in France. He was thinking that with those tokens he could introduce himself with the family, since he knew that Camille was the most difficult and jealous of Francesca's daughters and also because he wanted to get into certain unpleasant family matters and these small tokens would make it easier.

After giving Francesca a tour of the hotel like the gardens, the pools and the conference rooms and reception rooms, she reminded him that she had to pass by her house to change cloth and they had arranged to meet Camille and her family at noon to have lunch at Camille's house. It was Saturday. Francesca's shop was closed and Camille and her husband were not working.

CHAPTER X
MEETING CAMILLE

On the way to Camille's house, he told Francesca to be careful and not to let her emotions noticeable, specially her expression. He asked her to let him manage this problem to have a conversation with her son-in-law as a mature man to a young man and with the experience of the years. Besides that, maybe their child was not aware of what was going on.

—You have to smile and talk to your daughter and your granddaughter Angeline, I have my ways to take the conversation to the right place without offending. You told me that your son-in-law speaks English because he lived in England for a period of time. Anyways we Americans are famous for intervening in case of crisis.

Francesca had no other alternative but to smile after those words. He was dressed like a real American, like a simple Texan with boots with an eagle on it, jeans and a checked shirt in red and white. He was only missing the hat, the horse and the handkerchief tied around the neck. She dressed very discreet but always elegant.

At the beginning of the meeting there was a little bit of tension in the group. After that, the girl kept looking at Christopher and asked her grandmother:

—Who is this man and why is he dressed like that? They all laughed at the child's remark and the Grandmother answered her question.

—He is a very good friend of mine.

Then in the middle of the explanation he spoke and told the girl that he was her "fiancée" a word that is also used in English as well as in French, then the girl asked:

—Is this man going to be my grandfather?

—That's what he wants; answered the grandmother.

Christopher didn't know what was going on but the tension was gone and they all laughed again. The girl kept starring at him like if he was in disguise. He got a little box out of his shirt's pocket and told the girl:

—Close your eyes and give me a hand. The grandmother translated for the little girl. Then the girl told her grandmother that her dad was teaching her English and asked Christopher:

—Hey, cowboy, why do I have to close my eyes and give you a hand?

—It is a surprise! Then she answered:

—Allright! And closed her eyes.

He put a very nice girl's watch that he had bought at the hotel shop in her hands. When the girl saw the watch started jumping.

—Look! What I wanted a Minnie Mouse's watch.

He bent to look at the watch in her wrist and she gave him a kiss on his cheek.

—Thank you, thank you, Fiancée.

Camille changed the way she was looking at him and her husband offered him something to drink. Christopher looked at him and spoke to him in English.

—There is nothing as wonderful as making a child happy. At the same time he was looking at the house and asked the son-in-law:

—Did you have to make a big sacrifice to construct such a beautiful home and a family?

Camille's husband answered:

—Yes, there was a lot of sacrifice from both of us. Instead of going out to dinner we ate at home. Instead of going to the movies we rented movies to watch at home and instead of going on vacations we spent that time in painting and decorating the house. If it wasn't for my mother-in-law who

helped us many times it wouldn't have been possible.
Christopher answered:

—God permits that you can enjoy it.

Francesca asked her' granddaughter to go next doors to show the watch to her friend and went to get Camille's gift with her and took the box of Cuban cigars out of a bag, so that Christopher could give it to her son-in-law, who got real happy with his Cigars and told him that it had been quite a while since he had one of those. He smoked one cigar when his daughter was born, that he bought a box of cigars to celebrate with the family. In France it was very expensive, only for the rich. They went to the terrace to smoke the Cigars and have coffee while women were making plans about where to go for lunch.

Christopher asked Francesca's son-in-law what was his name. My name is Alain-he responded. Then he on turn asked Christopher for his name and asked him where was he from. This last question, he promised to answer some other day. Alain suspected that this was not just a visit, that there was a purpose. Christopher asked him about his profession, and said, I heard that you are an Industrial Chemist and worked for an industry for the making of paints, and continued:

—It should be an interesting job because you have to be experimenting with new products.

Alain answered with another question:

—What do you do in the United States?

—I am an investor, I distribute tires at an international level and have invested in real estate properties.

—Then, you are economically solid? —insisted Alain.

—More or less, but, let's get to the bottom of this. My respects to your opinion ends when I intend to get involved in yours, please give me the privilege to introduce myself in your personal life. Francesca told me what is going on in this family. I would like to talk to you, please do not interrupt me. This home that you have both built, with sacrifice, where you sacrificed youth and economy to get to this. You had a daughter as proof of your love for each other from this union. A very pretty and smart girl that looks a lot like you. Christopher continues:

—When you met your wife twelve years ago, she was pretty and young. Am I right? And you discard her now like an old rag. If this happens in reverse, would you like it? Of course not. Would you like to lose the love of your child and have her under the roof of another man, whom you don't know what would be capable of. Everything for a younger vagina? You don't realize what you are doing? We Americans are famous for being rude and too direct and you will have to excuse my honesty, but on the long run, we all do the same in a bed, more or less, but the same. You will destroy your family and all that you have achieved. You will lose it for a whim. When you look back and realize what has become of your home you will regret it, and your wife will never trust you. I have taken the liberty of talking to you like this because I believe that God brings a person to your life for a reason. He sends Angels and emissaries, that is my mission here today.

Alain responded to all his commentaries and asked him to let him explain now:

—Maybe you have not woken up at home with the screaming of a wife; sometimes she even pulls the child by the hair to make her hurry to school, because it's getting late and the problem is that my wife doesn't like to get up early. She goes out like a mess, she doesn't take care of her diet and doesn't have a gesture of love with me, because she says that she is too tired from working all day. It has been a long time that there is no sex between us. Do you consider this to be a home or hell? Did you listen to me? Please tell me what you think about this.

—Alain, let me tell you. You need to take a stand as the head of this family, you have to let your wife know how disappointed you are with her attitude and pray together. Ask God for help to get you out of this turbulence of hate and passion. All can be resolved. Would you accept an invitation for a vacation to the United States so that you can see several places? The girl can stay with her grandmother and I in my house and on the way back from that trip you take her to Walt Disney World parks and that way she can personally meet Mickey Mouse. I will pay all of the expenses and don't feel bad, I do it for the child. Do you authorize me to have a conversation with your wife? I am going to be very crude with her. Alain answered to his proposal:

—Of course, you are a good man, but I wish you luck because she is not easy.

Christopher went to see Francesca and Camille and talking to Francesca he said:

—I need you to help in translating my conversation with Camille, ask her that if it is OK with her I would like to talk to her for a little while. I already spoke to her husband, who was very receptive and open with me. Please explain all these to your daughter because I want to invite her to a vacation with her family to the US and I would also talk to her about other things of interest to her. Tell her that I also have a daughter and I am her counselor and not to look at me as a stranger because I have the best of intentions.

Francesca was talking to Camille for a few minutes and then Francesca told Christopher that Camille was receptive. He looked at her eyes to see if she was honest and observed her Trachea to observe if she was sincere or not.

—Please Camille, let me know what your interests are in life?

Let me know what worries you the most.

—My husband, this separation, that I can see you know about. My daughter and the repercussion that this separation might have in her personality, I am also worried about my mother, who is no longer a young woman and I do not want to give her worries. That is why I had not told her about what I am going through —she responded.

—Camille, my girl, please let me know if you feel responsible for this problem. If you have some regrets. Well, let me know what made you come to this end.

Camille responded:

—No, I don't feel guilty, it is him who has another woman. He is an awful man an egotist that only thinks about himself.

—What is the first thing that you do in the morning when you wake up besides washing yourself? At what time do you get up and at what time do you have to be at work? How long is the trip from home to work?

—I wake up at 7:30 and I have to be at work at 9:00.

-It takes me 40 minutes to get to work.

—What this means is that you only have 30 minutes to get ready, have breakfast and take care of your husband and your daughter. I don't think that 30 minutes is enough for your occupations, taking care of personal hygiene, getting pretty, help your daughter get ready and take care of your husband, have a breakfast in family, talk to the girl, ask your husband about his work issues or about any other matters. You are probably asking yourself what am I doing asking you so many questions, or, like that Cuban saying:

"Who has given me a candle to light in this burial?" But, it is very simple. I love your mother! and her worries are my worries.

—The day your mother and I decide to be together. Her daughters' problems are going to be my problems. You still are a very pretty and young girl, but I do not know if you are depressed, or have another problem, but it is evident that you have abandoned your image and have forgotten more important details of yourself. If it is necessary, to recover your family, you must seek professional help. Maybe there is something that worries you and you don't know have to express it.

He continued talking:

—Love is not receiving, you must also give love. When you give you receive and who loves, wants his mate to be happy with you. You don't need a school to learn how to caress your lover. A woman has to be a wife, a lover and a friend and at the end when alone with your husband you have to become a prostitute so that he doesn't look for another woman. So that he gets home and compares and realizes that he doesn't have a magazine model at home, but a woman that is aging by his side but that is worth a lot more than that other woman, but, first of all, she is the mother of his child and loves him.

—The first thing a woman must do when she wakes up is praying for her family, then washing herself then go to bed and give her husband a kiss. If she has to sacrifice one hour of sleep, she has to do it, because that kiss in the morning is very important. A woman must be seductive and sensual. Then, dedicate 15 minutes to dress up pretty. Christopher continued talking nonstop.

—You are beautiful but you don't even take good care of your hair. You have not realized that you came to this world as a woman, but, not to be diminished or mistreated, but, you have to work on your personality and act like a woman, mother and wife. You are a very attractive and smart woman and, I am not reprimanding you, I am counseling because of the experience of my years and some knowledge in Psychology. You are depressed and you think that you have lost this fight. When I spoke to your husband he complained about your fights and screaming since you wake up. Do you know why you do it? Because you have not dedicated the amount of time you need to attend your chores.

—The girl annoys you because you don't have time for her. She probably suffers from the fighting and screaming in the mornings. There is no time for her, there is no time for kissing and caring for your husband in the morning and at bedtime. There is no time for a long bath, perfuming and putting on an attractive night gown to be with your husband, nor to dress properly in the morning to go to work and not even time to have coffee or juice with your family. You are missing all of this for sleeping a little bit longer. Remember that the day will come when you will sleep eternally and then you will see how much you missed when alive.

Christopher talked to her like if he was talking to his own daughter:

—You cannot give up. You have a family, a daughter that if your marriage falls apart will have to spend her youth with a stranger that when she is fully developed, might even look at her with desire looking at her young body and can even try to touch her.

—As I previously told you and told Alain, I want to give you the gift of that vacation for the privilege of being a part of your family.

Christopher kept talking and told Camille that he knew that she was always buying good cloth for Angeline, but, that instead of helping her putting them on, she screams at her and pulls her hair because she is always in a hurry, what makes that pretty cloth lose its value. It is preferable not to buy anything because you will not regain her love that way. Hug her, kiss her, caress her and touch that beautiful hair that she has, even if you have to sacrifice a few more hours of your time. Throw yourself on the floor to play with her, pretty soon she will be a woman and you will not be able to do it.

—I believe that both of you need to sacrifice two hours every day instead of one, because one hour will only let you take care of yourself and fixing a perfumed bedroom that would invite to make love in. After your daughter goes to bed try to be a seductive woman like you probably used to do when you met. You have broken those ties of affection. There is something in your past that has been bothering you because I see it in your eyes. If you want to talk about that with me, something that we cannot do alone because I need an interpreter, I am ready to listen to your problem. Camille started crying and told him:

—Christopher, my husband have never wanted to have any more children with me. I lost a pregnancy some years ago and I don't know if he is traumatized because of that incident or it is that he does not want a big family with me. I am tired of asking him over and over and he has not agreed.

—I was talking to your husband and he complains of the lack of patience that you have with your daughter and that is the reason why he has not wanted any more children with you. Having an only child is difficult for you to handle, he might think you are not fit for two kids. Please seek

Physiologic or religious help and you will be able to win this battle. I am going to call your husband, not for a discussion but to seek an alliance of love between the two of you and you will find out if he is interested in saving his home.

Alain came over and formed part of the group and was eager to listen to all she had said.

Christopher talking to Alain, told him that he would also have to help in the morning getting the child ready for school and cooperate with Camille in some of the morning chores, such as fixing the bed with her.

Then, when Alain saw Camille's tears coming out of her eyes he said:

—I agree, I will try. And you?

—Of course, I will.

Then they hugged and kissed. She went to get cups to cheer with champagne. The cups were dusty of lack of use and Francesca had to wash them. They were so happy that Francesca told her son-in-law to talk to Christopher and ask him how to use the Champaign that was left after drinking. Christopher and Francesca began laughing at her remark. Then Angeline came over and got in between her father and her mother, she looked at them very surprised because they were embracing each other and told them.

—I am very happy with my wrist watch and my parents together!

—Alain told Camille that they were going to accept the Gringo Grandpa's offer to take a trip to the United States within approximately 30 days, date in which they would all be on vacation from work.

Camille didn't lose time and with her mind fixed in a possible pregnancy, asked Alain:

—Are you ready to have another child once we have

settled our issues?

—Christopher wanted to add a few words:

—Please remember that the best gift is to give the person you love a hug and tell him "whatever we go through I will always be with you" and then, do it. Do you agree Alain?

Francesca and Christopher were more at ease, with the three of them together. Francesca was smiling and kissing Christopher. He asked her:

—Do you want to take a Champagne bath?

—No, bathe me with kisses, it's not a matter of champagne. Not only have you gotten me out of my enclosure and solitude, but, you have brought love to my life and on top of that you have helped in the recovery of my daughter's happiness and you have cared for my granddaughter, it's me that owes you a champagne bath.

Christopher still worried, told Francesca:

—It has been a very intensive day fighting the enemy because you couldn't feel the presence of God when we arrived at your daughter's house. Sometimes God brings us back what we had lost, and gives you what you need at the right time. Maybe your husband was better than me, but I brought you back to life. Regarding your daughter and family, there is a lot of praying to be done, but talking about us, we have to eat now because and I am very hungry. With cheese pieces and sweets you cannot satisfy a 6-foot tall man.

—So sad, she answered, that we never went to have lunch with them. We have to invite them some other day.

—What do you want to eat Francesca? Because I want to eat caviar, strawberries and chocolate and a French woman for dessert.

Then they went to a restaurant, after dinner he proposed going back to the hotel, but, she said no. I don't want silk sheets or feather pillows but I have a home for both of us. Then, he asked her:

—Are you telling me that this is for all of our lives?

Do you accept to be my wife?

—Not yet, I have certain things to take care of before getting there.

He kept quiet and thinking a lot but, after that he went to her house. They made love to each other like adolescents looking which were the most passionate demonstrations of love that would make each other happy, it was an intense night. After making love they fell profoundly asleep.

The following morning Francesca prepared a big exquisite breakfast for them.

—Are you also a good cook? asked Christopher joking and brought her body against his by the back, kissing her neck and shoulders by the stove. She was complaining but she was happy to have him in her kitchen. After breakfast they kissed and then he left for the hotel and told her that he would go change cloth and be back in less than two hours. Please get very pretty, he told her, since they only had two days left to enjoy his most delighted sight, who was her.

CHAPTER XI
LAST OUTTING IN PARIS

Christopher went back to his room and changed cloth for some very comfortable attire to go visit the Seine, a river in Paris.

She was also changing cloth, this time she chose tight jean pants, a shirt, high tight boots and a handkerchief around her neck. She dressed as an American Cowboy Girl, all which looked very good on her and she felt very proud to dress like him. They took a taxi to the river. When Christopher saw the river he was very impressed for its wideness and beauty and bridges of immense altitude and edifications at both sides of the river, all of which were built over a century ago and of beautiful designs and the reflection of the buildings in the water.

When passing in front of the Notre Dame Cathedral they realized that its architectural design was unique and astonishing. They traveled in a tourist's boat called "Pont Alexandre III". Christopher wouldn't lose the opportunity to touch Francesca everywhere he could and she did not stop asking him to stop because they were in public.

—I thought this country was one of the most liberals in the world, he said. I want to put it to work.

She told him not to do certain things because she was not part of the liberal era and the only thing she hasn't done this time is to take her cloth off and make love to him on top of the boat.

—I wish I could.

—Not me. There are forty people on this boat.

—Yes, but there is an old man looking at us and is having of lot of fun, looking at my hands.

—I am a sixty-year-old woman and not an adolescent.

—My love, he replied, I opened the "Passionate Pandora

Box" in you. What are you going to do when I am gone? I rather buy you a sex gadget so that you don't make love to anybody else until I am back.

—Christopher, are you sane or did you have alcohol when leaving the hotel? First, touching me in front of 40 persons and now talking about buying me a sex gadget when I have never used one and don't intend to do so at this age.

—Oh, Francesca! You are living in the past century. I want you to know that the statistics show that 2 billion of those toys have been sold in the United States. The approximate price of one those is between $20.00 and $30.00, if you divide that by 2 billion you will realize that most of the women in the country use one of those and the Statistics include people from everywhere including France. I will tell you a joke about those toys. Do you want to hear it? There was a young lady who had one of those in a drawer in her room. Her dad went to fix the drawer and found the toy. Then, he asked her:

—Daughter, what is this?

—Don't worry dad, this is my husband.

—What are you saying? your husband?

—Yes daddy. I don't have to iron or wash cloth for this husband, I don't cook for him, he does what I want and when I want, without any questioning and I am safe from contacting a transmitted decease.

—My child, looking at it from that point of view, I will accept it because you are not a minor and you decide your destiny.

Several days later the daughter found her father with the toy on top of the table and drinking a beer.

—Daddy! What are you doing with that toy?, then he responded.

—I am having a beer with my son-in-law.

Francesca had a laughed uncontrollably and everybody looked at her. The old man across from them was surprised with her laugh and then she said.

—I have my little crazy American back.

Then she suggested going to eat something fast.

—You saw the river and I want to go to a theater, then Christopher responded:

—Do I take my pillow?

—Pillow? Those plays are magnificent, don't act like an illiterate. I am taking you to see "The Miserables", a very famous play.

—No, this illiterate already read the book by Victor Hugo. Is there a play showing in a burlesque theater?

—Are we back to the same craziness?

—Ok, it's all right, I will go to see the play, but I am taking my pillow.

—Don't you dare take a pillow!

—Ok, I am hungry. What do we eat?

—Not now, take a small snack at the hotel and I will do the same in my apartment, because if you eat too much you will fall asleep at the theater.

—I have to choose the cloth I am taking to the theater. What do you want me to wear, a tuxedo or a suit?

—Whatever you want.

When he picked her up in a limousine wearing a tuxedo and Yanay saw him, she exclaimed:

—Francesca, look who is here, if you don't want him I will take him. That American is hot!

—Do you want to lose your job Yanay?

She was walking down the stairs with a dress made of Chiffon with an embroidered cloth on top in emerald green, low neck slightly showing her breasts. She was wearing her pearls and emerald necklace with a very thin crown putting her hair up, a small purse covered with faux pearls and matching shoes. Then he exclaimed:

—Looking at you I have confirmed that you are a dress designer and also a porcelain doll by Lladro in colors, with your beautiful mother of pearl color skin and your distinguished features. Yanay also commented that she looked like a queen when she was walking towards the limousine and the driver was opening the door for her. By the door of the limousine Christopher started talking out-loud:

—This woman is mine, mine, and only mine and no one else's. Look how pretty she is.

Francesca got into the Limousine in a rush and said:

—Oh my God, how crazy he is! I am ashamed.

—Francesca, to be with me you don't have to be crazy but it helps!

When they entered the theater, they called the attention of many people. She looked beautiful and he was not far behind, he was very elegant, they arrived in a limousine and those people entering the theater kept asking themselves if they were famous or jet setters. They had reservations for a balcony in a very visible place. They could hear the actors very well. Christopher who was not a fan of theater plays was constantly interrupting Francesca's attention by contemplating her beauty and elegance and telling her all sorts of compliments and she kept asking him to talk in a lower voice, not so loud.

—Wouldn't you rather that I brought the pillow? Ok, my love, just to make you happy I will pay attention to the play, but, haven't you heard that North Americans are more into sports, it's our nature, we are like that.

When the play finished they went to the hotel and all of the guests looked at her to admire her beauty.

They went to his hotel room and they talked about many subjects. He explained to her that as soon as he got to the United States he would start obtaining a Visa for her.

Christopher had asked the hotel to dress the bed in red sheets, incense and candles around the bed, because it was the last night together until next time. Before going to bed he asked her for a dance, "naked", to dance a song by Whitney Houston, "I will always love you". He played the song and sang near her ear. It was premonition of what was coming, the song goes in her most important lyrics like this:

"If I could stay it would have to be on your way, so, that I will leave but I know I will think of you in all of my doings and I will always love you, I will always love you, Oh, my love, your memories is all I am taking with me, so bye please don't cry. I will always love you, I will always love you. My feelings for you are so strong that I need you to give me all of you, with all your passion."

They continued dancing to the same song and she also murmured to his ear.

—You want me to give you all of me with all my senses. What have I done so far? Can't you feel that I have given me to you without reserve, without prejudice or inhibitions?

She continued...

—At my age, I never imagined having experimented a tremendous passion, and you are asking me to give myself in with all my senses? There is nothing more in me that I can give you, you have taken it all. All of my body without any little place, now I am going to the hall and will start screaming the same way you did in front of my business.

—Do you see that man there, that is my man, can you see how handsome he is?

—See, I am the crazy one now.

—Francesca, I am starting to fear you, you have gotten

contagious by me.

—This is the most delicious craziness that I have experimented in my life. If this is being crazy, please let me be and let's not lose any more time and let's go and get into the red bed sheets so that we get contagious by the passion of the color.

After an intense love making experience, they got tired and fell asleep until morning. They had only ten more hours to be together. They went to have breakfast to the restaurant in the hotel and then he called a taxi and told her that he would pick her up between 2:00 and 3:00 p.m. to have lunch together and then go to the airport. He had to spend many hours in a flight and didn't like eating in the airplane because he got nervous while flying for a long period of time. When Francesca got to her shop Yanay told her:

—Lady! Good to see you. How was the night? I see you are looking younger.

—It's that I am very happy and realized as a woman and that makes me feel younger, I am living unimaginable moments.

—Oh my lady, just by listening to you all the hairs in my head stood up, even my teeth felt it, by the way, one of your ears is bleeding.

—It is true, this man cannot caress me when dancing, he also bites me.

—How exciting.

—Well, I have to get dressed, he is picking me up in a bit to have lunch and then go to the airport.

When Christopher was getting closer to her business in the taxi, a tremendous car accident occurred a few blocks from the shop and he decided to get the baggage and walk with it because time was of the essence. He was walking by the other side of the street when he saw Francesca kissing and hugging a tall brunette handsome pretty young man and besides hugging her he was embracing her and then they got inside the building holding hands. Then, he saw the man through the window but couldn't see her.

The rage, the pain and the impotence at that sight drove him blind, up to a point that if he would have had a gun on him at that time would have committed a big mistake. He closed his eyes, thought about his family with a big pain inside. He felt his heart breaking into pieces. With tears coming out of his eyes he started walking back to find a taxi that would take him back to the hotel. When he arrived at the hotel the boy at the front desk asked him:

—Sir, didn't you leave and check out already?

—No, there has been an inconvenience, I am not going back to the room, but I will have coffee and I need a favor from you. I need paper and an envelope and I need you to take that envelope to a place I will tell you. Please accept these $50.00 as my appreciation for this favor.

—You don't have to do that, you have been very splendid with me while your stay at the hotel.

Christopher took the paper and envelope and with a coffee and pill for the blood pressure he started writing a letter to Francesca:

"Francesca, it is not necessary for you to accompany me to the airport, I know that you are in your bedroom in good company. I never imagined how fake you were. I took you to a pedestal and now I see you insultingly dismissive, I never thought you were hiding another man in your life. You have provoked a very profound pain in me. You were my present and my future. I didn't know that I was a stupid dreamer that was being betrayed. I have been a joke for all of you. I saw you hugging and kissing with a brunette man, younger than us, right in front of your

business and after that you went to your bedroom holding hands. Where I slept with you the day before and you totally gave yourself in to me.

Don't look for me, don't call, forget that I exist. I have changed to an earlier flight and I don't see myself setting foot in this land ever again.

Christopher

When Francesca received the letter, she read it and told Yanay:

—Yanay, please get me a taxi as soon as possible.

She was crying, very nervous and with her hands trembling while holding the letter. She made a sudden turn in the stairs, to go and get her purse, but she put her foot in the wrong place and fell back downstairs. When she got to the end of the stairs she had lost consciousness and then Yanay started screaming, very nervous and asked a customer to call an ambulance to take her to the nearest emergency room.

CHAPTER XII
FRANCESCA'S ACCIDENT
Hopitaux Universitaires Paris Centre

As soon as the ambulance got to the hospital the paramedics started working on her, because the accident had been extremely serious. Yanay asked the paramedics to let her accompany her in the ambulance to the nearest hospital, but the paramedics explained that they had to take her to a hospital with a trauma center, even if it was further away. Yanay was still very nervous. Crying and trying to get in touch with Francesca's daughters, first Camille, the nearest daughter and then Chloe in Nice. She kept explaining over and over that it had been a tremendous fall because she rolled down the stairs on her back. The paramedics talked between them and were communicating with the hospital and had administered oxygen and an IV. But the paramedics kept moving their heads with disappointment because of the seriousness of the situation. Yanay kept telling the daughters that she was in shock, to please go to the hospital and to call their brother to have him come to the hospital as well, since she didn't have his telephone number.

They finally arrived and at the hospital, there were two nurses at the hospital waiting for her. They immediately took her to the trauma center. Once inside the hospital Yanay was asked to stay in the lobby, to help with the patient's information. Also, they asked her if she was present when the accident occurred. She responded that she was present with a gesture of her head. Yanay was offered a glass of water and was asked if she wanted a pill to relax her nerves.

Every time a nurse or doctor came out of the center Yanay would approach them and asked them about

Francesca's condition. She was not given much information until the chief nurse of the department asked her:

—Are you related to the patient?

—Not really but she is like a mother to me. She is all I have in this country. The daughters should be arriving any time, but, please let me know how she is doing.

—We are working on her, the best trauma doctor is taking care of her, she is constantly being monitored, we have put ice packs on top of her head, we are monitoring her blood pressure, respiration and the heart. We have her on oxygen and we are doing our best for her not to get worse. We have also called the best Neurosurgeon who has ordered several tests and an MRI of the brain and another one of the whole body. We have to wait for the results and then the doctor will come out and talk to the family.

The first minutes seemed eternal. Camille just got to the hospital with her husband who had left work. Yanay asked them about the child and she was told that they left her with a neighbor. Camille started asking Yanay about the whereabouts of the accident.

—How is it possible that something like this happened after so many years living in the same apartment?

Camille and her husband kept asking themselves where was Christopher when it happened.

—Christopher, where is Christopher? Camille asked Yanay.

—I wished I knew, answered Yanay, Francesca was waiting for him to go the airport and instead, an employee of the hotel showed up with a letter and she was very agitated while reading the letter, -she asked me to call a taxi and then she fell down the stairs.

Camille asked her husband to call the hotel to find out

if something had happened to him or if they knew about his destiny, because at this time he should have already been in the airplane back to the United States.

A while after that, Alain came back very disappointed and told Camille that he was told that Christopher had left the hotel early that day and that he had made arrangements to take an earlier flight. The last they saw of him was having a coffee at the hotel restaurant and writing a letter, before taking a taxi. Alain said:

—I hope not, God forbid that he might have had bad news from his family and never contacted Francesca.

Camille asked her husband to go back home to take care of their daughter, feed her and take her to school and told him:

—I am going to stay all night. On your way home take Yanay to work because she mentioned that she doesn't remember if she closed the doors of the store or if she left it open, because she rushed to come in the ambulance with mom.

Yanay didn't want to leave the hospital, but Camille ordered her to leave and told her:

—Yanay, this is an order, please put a sign in the front door of the business and write that the business is closed for inventory. Rest tonight and come back tomorrow morning. Try to look for the letter my mom read and try to find the information of Christopher's phone, business, etc. so that I can locate him.

—All right, I will stay in Francesca's apartment, just in case Christopher or any of his relatives call. I don't see myself sleeping tonight, please Camille call me and let me know how she is doing.

Camille rested on a recliner at the hospital to wait for the doctors in case they asked for a relative. Camille called

Chloe very often, because since they were not that well off they drove instead of taking a train and that trip took several hours.

It was nearly 11:00 p.m. when Yanay got to the business, the first she looked for was the letter that was left over the dress that Francesca wore the night before to go to the theater. She felt very sad at the sight of the dress and started crying, she was very apprehensive when she saw the letter and kept making the sign of the cross in front of the letter and the dress. When she started reading the letter which was in Spanish Yanay was speechless, she didn't know whether to hide the letter or read it to the family until Francesca woke up and would tell her what to do. She kept asking herself. – Who was the man that was here today and I didn't see? Besides that, after so many years with her I never saw another man.

Then, she remembered that Alexander, Francesca's brother was at the store visiting that day to meet Francesca's boyfriend, because she mentioned it to her a couple of times that since Christopher was leaving that day to the United States she wanted her brother to meet him before he left France. She remembered Francesca and Alexander kissing hugging and going up to the apartment that day. What a horror; she thought, how is it possible that when Francesca found happiness, might have also found death? She made the sign of the cross several times again. I won't be able to sleep all night. She looked into Francesca's purse and found a business card in English with Christopher's name in the card, she went to bed and took the card and put it on her purse and slept with the letter and the card by her.

Yanay got to the hospital very early the following morning and took coffee and pastries for the family, and Chloe had already arrived and she found both sisters very sad and crying. They had already spoken to the neurosurgeon who told them that Francesca had suffered a brain contusion, that she was still unconscious. The x-rays reflected a small blood hemorrhage in the tissues of the brain, what indicated that there was a blood vessel inside the tissues and was creating inflammation and intracranial bleeding.

Also, the blood can also form a clot called epidural hematoma, in which event she would have to be taken to surgery. They were already getting ready to intervene and taking all of the necessary blood work. The doctor was positive that with surgery the blood hemorrhage could be stopped and then it all would take a long period of recuperation, but, he could give them an approximate total of 70% recovery.

During the recovery process she will suffer headaches, vomiting, instability, high blood pressure and lack of vision at some point, but, then all will slowly go to the normal stages. They asked the doctor what they could do and he responded that they would have to pray for her and for him so that he could do a good job. After surgery they would need to take turns to rest afterwards because it will be a long period of recuperation.

Yanay was quiet, she gave them coffee and pastries and sat in a chair to wait for them to eat. The neurosurgeon had told them that surgery would approximately take five to six hours to be able to stop the bleeding before closure.

Francesca's brother arrived and then Yanay remembered that she had the letter and card in her purse and gave him the letter to read. He was extremely disappointed after reading the letter and told them:

—I cannot believe I could have caused so much pain to the

the person I love the most.

Yanay on turn said:

—I knew all along that the American who saw himself as a king was stupid.

Alain jumped and said:

—No Yanay, you are wrong. We men react like animals upon a sight like that. We are not very rational. If I would have been in his place, I might even have thrown them both down the stairs.

Alexander agreed:

—I would have also done the same.

Then Alain explained that it was 2:00 p.m. in the United States and since he spoke English he was going to contact Christopher, to let him know what was happening and also clarify that he was wrong, that the man he saw was her brother.

CHAPTER XIII
CHRISTOPHER'S ARRIVAL, BALTIMORE, MARYLAND

Christopher went directly from the airport to his house and called his children to ask for their whereabouts and the businesses, the tires and the rentals and some other issues. His son told him that one of their truck drivers had been involved in an accident a couple of days ago and the truck was declared total loss. Many tires got lose and they lost approximately 60 tires. Fortunately, the driver was alive, but that he had a few fractures and was hospitalized in stable condition.

—Please Richard, do not leave his family unattended. Keep paying his salary and whatever else they might need, said Christopher.

I will see you in a few days. I am going to our cabin by myself. I want to meditate for a few days and spend those days in tranquility. The children got worried and asked him if he had problems in France during his stay, because he was always saying that he was very happy. Since they were in a conference call, his daughter, told him that his tone of voice worried her, seemed like he was omitting details and also asked:

—Is it that you do not confide us?

But he asked them not to worry that he only wanted to be quiet for a few days.

Christopher got to the Cabin. He had driven his truck for several hours, thinking about Francesca's dishonesty on the way. He kept talking to himself, kept repeating himself: I consider myself a kind man and a patient man. I have forgiven many times other people's mistakes, but, in this instance I cannot forgive her or go back with her.

My father was right, when he said that the only loved

ones you can trust are those of God and your parents. Maybe my destiny is to spend my life alone, I am not afraid of loneliness but I fear betrayal and the pain it brings with it. I am full of negative and sad thoughts and he kept driving for another four hours like that.

After a long ride and very tired, he arrived to his destination. Crying he brought the food down and the fishing accessories. He cried because of Francesca's betrayal and also because of what getting to this place meant to him, where he spent so much time with his deceased wife. Where he enjoyed many days of resting, love and peace. This contributed to make him feel worse.

The first thing he did when he entered the cabin was to look for a musical record with mellow music that could get Francesca's image hugging another man out of his mind. He had taken a box of records from his bedroom and took it with him. When he started listening to the record he did not recognize the song. Then a famous Spanish Singer started singing the lyrics:

"Remember the days we had, the moments that you spent, remember, how we felt in love,
Francesca, don't leave me, my Francesca.
Don't leave me, I beg you, If you know I cannot live if your love is not for me.
Francesca, don't leave I beg you my Francesca, if you known I cannot live if your love is not for me".

He couldn't believe what he was listening to or if it was a joke of a very bad taste, or, that he had taken the music box of his maid that would only listen to music in Spanish. What a horror! I cannot believe I am listening to a song dedicated to a certain Francesca, what kind of game from destiny is this? And out loud he said, I will finish this joke right now. Both, the record and Francesca are going to hell.

He got the record and threw it against the floor and then started stepping on it. He was out of control.

Then, he decided to prepare some coffee while he cleaned the cabin, he changed the bed sheets which had not been changed in a very long time. When he finished, took a shower and threw himself in bed. He didn't wake up for a long time, until he heard a noise of something or someone walking around the cabin and through the window he saw a bear and further from the cabin a deer. The bear was looking for food on the back of his truck attracted by the smell of food that he had transported in the vehicle. He fixed himself a sandwich and drank a glass of milk. He got some more coffee to spend the night, but, had to turn the electric plant on to be able to watch some television, started refrigerator on and put some other things to work. He had to throw two warning shots to the air to make the bear leave. He went to town the following day to buy some things he needed and to make a call to the business to find out how the employee that had the accident was doing and to talk to his children to let them know how he was doing, since he saw them worry when he left.

Telephone call to Christopher at his Business from France

Around 3:00 p.m., U. S. Time, an urgent long distance call to Christopher Smith was received at his business' phone. As the operator announced to the girl that answered. The receptionist replied:

—One moment please, I will page his son at the warehouse and will put him on. The waiting time will take a few minutes, please don't hang up.

She started calling Richard through the loud speakers to let him know that he had an urgent phone call waiting from France. Richard rushed to the phone.

—I am Christopher's son and my name is Richard. Who is calling and what is the emergency?

—I am Alain, Francesca's son-in-law.

—And, who is Francesca may I ask?

—Your father's fiancée.

—What's happening?

—Francesca had an accident at home and she is at the hospital.

—I am going to relay the message to my father, because my father is not with us, he has left to our cabin, far from here, apparently he came back from France feeling pretty bad and went away for a while.

—Richard, please listen. There has been a huge misunderstanding. Please try to contact your father, he misinterpreted some affectionate hugs and kisses between Francesca and her brother. Your father saw them and thought otherwise. Her brother, is with us at the hospital and is desperate to explain what really happened to your father and the purpose of his visit. When Christopher went to pick her up to go to the airport he saw them hugging as I told you. Your father went blind and didn't even get near them. I don't criticize him because I would have probably reacted the same way, added Alain. Christopher went back to the hotel blaming Francesca of infidelity and when she received a letter brought by a hotel's employee she ran stairs up to get her purse and go to the hotel to clarify the situation, but, a bad step made her fall down the stairs.

—What a disgrace, my God. I will immediately rush to the Cabin to pick my dad up because the trip to the Cabin takes several hours. I will call my sister on my way there and I will ask her to buy a ticket back to France as soon as possible, because he can also be very ill and we are also worried about him.

—Please Alain, give me your phone number so that my father can get in touch with you and the name and address of the hospital. Is it in Paris?

—Yes, she is in Paris, in the University Hospital.

—Thank you very much, my father will get in touch with you. I will leave right now.

—OK, Richard, thank you so much for your courtesies.

Call to Milam:

—Millie, my sister. I know what is going on with Dad.
I am on my way to the cabin.

—What happened?

—I will tell you later in detail, but, he hasn't changed, he still is a rough American Cowboy. Please, I need you to go home, get his papers out of his briefcase and get him an urgent flight back to Paris, first class, very comfortable. We should be arriving to the airport in a matter of seven hours. Ask Nana to rearrange his luggage and pack it with new clean clothes.

—You cannot leave me like this, what happened?

—Please take this number down. It's Alain's, dad's fiancée's son-in-law, who speaks perfect English. Ask him and let him know that you are worried about her, and continued:

—The least that has happened because of Dad's lack of communication, is that the woman is in comma with a brain trauma.

—Oh! But, what happened? Did he hit her? I cannot believe it. My father has never been violent.

—No, Milam, no…! It was an accident.

—Ohhhhh…!, what a relief. I will call Alain right away.

She called Alain and told him to count on them for anything. Any additional charge will be born my by dad, and that they were also very worried. She also said that she was traveling with her dad, that she hadn't told him yet but that he was also feeling bad and needed their attention and help.

Richard arrived a little bit later than 7:00 p.m. to the Cabin. It was a beautiful sunset. Christopher was trying to concentrate on the TV but heard the motor of a vehicle nearby and looked through the window and he saw some lights getting closer. He kept looking and thought that it might be a neighbor who wanted to greet him or the sheriff that was riding around to take a look at the properties.

Richard's truck braked all of a sudden by the cabin, making the dust and dead leaves fly. Christopher kept wondering who approached his cabin in such a manner when he saw Richard getting off the car in a rush. Christopher ran to the door. What happened Richard? You got here like a crazy person, and added:

—Has anything happened?

—Yes, something horrible has happened.

—Is it your sister or the truck driver?

—No. It happened to your fiancée.

—What fiancée are you talking about? I don't have one.

—Yes, you do. Her name is Francesca and she is in a comma in a hospital in Paris because of your bad temper and stupidity.

—What's wrong with you? You are talking to your father, respect me and explain what happened to that woman.

—Get your medication and take everything of importance with you, I will disconnect the electric plant and close all doors to the cabin. Dad, we have to be in our way to the airport as soon as possible. I will explain the details in the truck but the only thing that I can say is that the man she was hugging and kissing is her brother that had come from a distant place to meet you.

—Her brother, of course, like if I am going to believe that.

—Dad, her son-in-law called me and told me that she received an offensive letter and when she went upstairs to her apartment to run after you with the letter in her hand she fell down the stairs hitting her head. She has a trauma in her brain and she is in very serious condition.

Christopher started crying, passing his hands over and over through his head and hitting the floor and asking God why was this happening to him. First he lost his wife in a very tragic manner and then this woman whom he also loved. He thought God had given him a second chance to be happy and he is also taking her away from him, then screaming:

—No, no, no, I will not permit having her taken, she is mine, I will fight for her life!

—Let's move fast Richard, let's go now!

—Dad. I love you, but I am very worried.

— Let's go, Richard, let's go. I am driving my truck, I will see you at the airport.

—You are coming with me dad, your truck is older, you use it for the boat and I will not see you fit to drive at this time.

—Richard, do you have Alain's number in France?

—Yes, I have his cell number and his international code because he gave it to me. I also gave it to my sister.

—And, why did you give that number to your sister?

—She is coordinating your arrival with that family and is also buying you the airplane ticket so that you don't have to wait in line. She is also taking your luggage to the airport.

—I can see that you have put me in a place of an old incompetent old man.

—No, Dad. It's not that.

—Don't try to outsmart me, at my 60 years of age I am stronger than you, more competent than a young man, sexually speaking and with more knowledge.

—Let's leave it like that, Super Senior. Hum, let's prove that when Francesca recovers.

—Ask her who I am…O.K. Please give me Alain's cell number and by the way give me your cell because mine has no battery.

He called Alain several times but he didn't answer, he was getting very impatient when Alain answered:

—Hello, Hello! Alain, it's me Christopher, I know what happened. Let me know how she is doing. What has the doctor told you?

—Not much, she is out of surgery but she is still in recovery and the neurosurgeon has not gotten out of the room. My wife and Chloe are there with Yanay waiting, but there are no news yet.

—Alain, I am on my way to the airport. I should arrive at 4:00 a.m. France's time. I will take my cloth to the hotel and leave to the hospital getting there around 6:00 a.m., I need you to talk to the hospital and ask for the best private room it has. I will pay for the expense, if there is one with a private waiting area ask for it. I will not move from her side until she has recovered. I will see you there and please ask her daughters to forgive me for acting so irresponsible.

Christopher wanted to drive because he was in a rush but Richard didn't let him drive.

—I will not permit an accident at this time, it would be the ultimate occurrence. Why don't you sleep in the car?

—Fall sleep now. Are you crazy? I will spend nine hours in the plane, there is plenty of time to sleep. If possible I will sleep for a little time, but, not even with a bottle of sleeping pills I will be able to do it. I am very tense and you have taken this opportunity to be irrespective.

—No Dad, I love you very much but it's that I was very nervous with the thought that you might have committed domestic violence with that woman.

—When have you known me to be such a violent individual? I never hit your mother nor I ever offended her, nor have I treated your grandmother badly, who was impossible and not my mother. I never told her that I regretted her actions to not hurt your mother's feelings.

—I don't know if I would have done the same thing you did. I would have to be on your shoes, said Richard.

They arrived to the airport around 11:30 at night and it was pouring.

—Dad, the flight is leaving at 2:00 in the morning and you should be arriving in Paris at 8:30 in the morning. You have time to get to the hotel, take a shower and get dressed before you leave for the hospital. Don't rush or go crazy because if you do, you lose more time.

When they arrived at Air France Departures, Milam was waiting for him with three suitcases. He kissed his daughter and gave her a big hug and asked her:

—Why so much luggage. I don't want to take a lot of cloth.

—No Dad, it's not your cloth. Two suitcases are mine and one is yours.

—Where are you going?

—I am going with you.

—Oh, my God, what the heck? You think that I am an old senile man.

—No, Dad. It's my obligation being with you at this time as your daughter to support you and try to make things easier with the French Family.

—The French woman's name is Francesca.

—What a beautiful name! said Milam.

—Richard please check-in. Take our luggage and find out which gate we have to take. We are going to have a coffee and I will have an apple pie. I haven't eaten and I have to take two pills for the headache because my head feels like it is going to break.

—No dad! Said Milam, let's go to the airport emergency room to have your blood pressure taken before we take the plane.

—Yes, yes, yes, I will go, but the coffee and apple pie first. Listen Babe, after I eat, take the pills and relax for a little while, the pain will go away.

—OK, Dad, you are impossible, but I adore you, said Milam.

A while later they heard flight number 399 going to Paris being called to Gate "G" to wait to board the plane. Christopher got close to his son and told him:

—My son, I miss you a lot when we are apart, but I need you to be in charge of the accident and the business and rents. I will send Milam back in six days.

Then Milam replied:

—You love to boss me around. You have already arranged for my return.

—No, my love, I don't want you at the hospital for so many days, this is not a trip of pleasure, when I marry Francesca you can come every month, if you wish.

—He is even talking about marriage, my dad is in big rush. Good for him!

They boarded the plane, the pills had already worked on Christopher's system and he slept a few hours. The Stewardess covered him with a blanket and Milam asked for a blanket for her and also slept a few hours with her head over her father's shoulder. When she got the blanket she asked the Stewardess not to wake her father up, that if they needed any information to please ask her. She looked at him and thought, this man is my idol. Christopher woke up at 6:00 in the morning, United States time. He woke Milam up to go together to the restrooms.

When they came back they were served champagne and were asked if they wanted something to eat, because the food was served two hours before they woke up. He did not want champagne, he wanted sprite and some crackers. Milam wanted something to eat because she was on an empty stomach and she was nauseous, probably her nerves, she thought.

Christopher turned the TV on and was thinking about the movies that won most of the Oscars in 2006, Babel, whose actors were Brad Pitt and Kate Blanchett. When the movie finished they tried to rest and the plane was ready to land. Fifteen minutes after that, they were asked to put the seat belts on; to sit straight and put all bags under the chairs to land.

Milam was sitting by the window and kept asking her dad to look, it was beautiful and all lights were on in the streets of the city and you can see the Eiffel Tower and there is a big amusement park by the tower. That is why Paris is known as "The City of Lights". What a beautiful sight! Captain Holden who was the chief of the crew told the passengers that he was happy to have them aboard.

CHAPTER XIV
ARRIVAL TO FRANCE

They took a taxi from the airport to the same hotel were Christopher stayed on the previous trip. Milam looked at the surroundings, WOW, she was in Paris, the City of her dreams, what ashamed that it is under these circumstances. The boy by the door immediately recognized him and welcomed him back, surprised because of his sudden return and with a young woman. Christopher told the kid that the young woman was his daughter who was staying for a few days with him. When he got to the desk he asked for a suite with two kingside beds for him and his daughter. It was after 4:00 a.m. and asked for two breakfasts with coffee in a rush, because they had to go out as soon as possible. Christopher asked the boy at the desk:

—Please get me the address and telephone number of the University's Hospital, because I have to urgently leave to the hospital. Milam, I don't think I will find Alain at this time at the hospital, he takes his daughter to school and is probably sleeping with her. Someone at the hospital might be able to help me interpret, either English or Spanish.

They got to the room, took a shower and got dressed, then Milam told him:

—Dad, let's have breakfast, take a pill and we go to the hospital. We are in Paris and it's difficult to find someone to understand you over the phone.

—OK, daughter! Call the front desk and ask them for a taxi to be here in 20 minutes to take us to the hospital.

We should have had a lighter breakfast.

Milam threw up all of her breakfast. She thought she was nervous to see her dad so worried. On the other hand, Christopher was worried as he could not understand his daughter's problem. Milam was pregnant but she was shy to confess that to her dad. She was aware that he had other worries to give him another one. She was very disappointed because the symptoms could show her pregnancy.

Two hours after breakfast she vomited again because she was feeling weak and had to eat breakfast again. When they arrived to the hospital Christopher went directly to the Recovery Room in the Surgery Department of the Trauma Center, he started inquiring for the patient named Francesca Lemar, and what room she was in. He asked in English and Chloe who was sitting in a corner of the room called him. His daughter told him:

—Daddy, there is a young girl calling you from that corner of this room.

Christopher immediately went to her and gave her a hug and a kiss. She understood very little Spanish and could not talk fluently to her, nevertheless, hugging her he kept asking for forgiveness for the situation that led to the accident. He told her that he felt responsible and this was the last thing he wanted to happen. Chloe, please call Yanay, said Christopher, while giving her his cellular.

They tried getting in touch with Yanay but she was so tired that couldn't hear the ring. They kept insisting until she grabbed the phone and she was a little bit sleepy but, Christopher was able to talk to her.

—Please Yanay! I need you here as soon as possible.
I am at the hospital.

—Has anything else happened? Is she doing well?

—I don't know. No one understands me and I don't speak French. I need you to ask when you get here and translate for me. I also need a private nurse to serve as interpreter for me, preferably someone that speaks English, because my daughter is accompanying me and she doesn't speak

French or Spanish. Please take a taxi. Call me when you are approaching the hospital.

—I will be there in less than an hour, don't get anxious. Then, Christopher saw a nurse coming out of the unit and asked Yanay to wait a minute:

—Please Yanay, there is a nurse here, I need you to talk to her, please ask her to give you an update of her condition and explain to the nurse that I am her fiancée and I need to stay with her.

When Yanay finished her conversation with the nurse, she told Christopher that Francesca was still in critical condition, that the Doctor would arrive to the hospital at 9:00 a.m. to evaluate the patient and read the charts of the nurses and doctors that worked in the night shift, that she was going to make an exception and would let him into the room for a little because at this stage any germ could be fatal.

The nurse took him to a room to change into sterile clothes. When the nurse took him to Francesca and he saw her unconscious, full of cables and monitors he got extremely impressed and his body began trembling. Tears ran down his face as he took one of her hands and kept repeating

—My love, it's Christopher, I am here, please forgive me, forgive me, I never meant to hurt you with that note and would have never wanted you go through all of this, please move the fingers of your hands to find out if you know that I am here. She did and he started crying like a child.

—The nurse with a sign of a finger, tried to tell him, "one hour". Also, pointed to the equipment in the room and moved her hand to express "don't touch". Finally, she brought him a chair so that he could sit next to her.

When the nurse left, he took Francesca's hands and

kissed them. Then, he took one of the hands and made it touch his face while he kept kissing her hand over and over and kept repeating, forgive me, forgive me and started praying like talking to God and asking for help. Please give me another opportunity, bring her back well like before and without any sequels. He spent quite a while praying. A doctor came into the room and asked him to leave the room. When leaving the room, he saw Yanay who informed him:

—Christopher, I just spoke to the attending physician and told me that the X-Rays don't show permanent injuries, that he is going to evaluate her progress. If the X-Rays were well taken, he believes that within 24 hours we will be able to see symptoms of improvement. He was very grateful with Yanay for being of help and offered to compensate her as soon as possible. Yanay's response was:

—She is like a mother to me and her improvement is my compensation.

—Fine, I understand, please let me introduce you to my daughter and I will interpret for her. She insisted in coming with me no matter what, but, it is going to be difficult for her because she doesn't speak French or Spanish. Yanay then suggested:

—I suggest that we contact a company of tourist mode here that there should be many contacts in this place of tourism and hire a guide or translator for you and your daughter, but mostly for her because I will stay here with you as long as possible so that you are informed about Francesca's condition.

—I need the interpreter here as soon as possible, to accompany my daughter all the time. I will not leave the hospital at any time.

Milam couldn't understand anything that they were

saying:

—Daddy, please ask this girl where we can find a place to pray and meditate.

Yanay asked the nurse, who informed her that taking the elevator to the first floor, to the left of the elevator in the lobby, you will find a Chaple. Christopher went down the elevator with his daughter and kneeled in front of a cross. Milam sat with Yanay in the other side of the chapel where there was an image of Virgin Mary. She kneeled in front of the Virgin and prayed to forbid her father from losing this opportunity to be happy and to bring Francesca back to the world and out of the darkness where she was. Milam also prayed for herself and to please guide her to find the way to get out of this problem she was going through. She didn't plan to abort the baby, she had already chosen a name and if the baby is a girl, she will name her Marie.

Yanay was observing Milam and noticed that as she prayed that she was touching her stomach. Then, she got more proximate to Milam and touching her belly, she asked:

—Baby? Milam got very nervous and put a finger on top her lips in a sign of silence. Yanay understood what was going on. When they went back to the intensive care unit, Camille and Alain were already there, Christopher felt more at ease and hugged them both, he kissed Camille and asked for forgiveness. She turned to him and through her husband, let Christopher know:

—Alain would have done the same, he has said it about four times already, don't suffer more for that, it was an accident, I know how much you love her.

Christopher and Alain separated from the girls.

—Alain, I need a big favor from you, I asked Yanay, but I believe you are better for the job and will do it faster. I need two English translators, one for my daughter, preferably a woman and another one for me, to stay with me here at the hospital. I know that it could be expensive but I get desperate when I don't understand what is going on, and added:

—Please don't leave right now, because the attending physician is reading the chart and the neurosurgeon is on his way and I need to talk to both of them; and continued:

—I need you to ask them not to worry about additional expenses if those are for her comfort and care, I will pay for all the expenses. I need you to go with my daughter when you hire to interpreters so that she can take the debit card with her to pay for that expense. I really appreciate all your help.

Alain responded that there was nothing to be grateful about his care, that this was his duty. All the group sat and spoke in different languages, no one understood the other. It was approximately 10:00 in the morning when the attending physician and the Neurosurgeon left the recovery room, the attending physician, the Neurosurgeon and a nurse approached them asking in French:

—Who are the relatives of patient Francesca? —all stood up and the physicians added—. Please, only the husband the children. Alain had to join the group in order to interpret for Christopher, explaining that he did not speak French. The neurosurgeon started explaining, as follows

—Fortunately, the tests do not reveal permanent damage, but, we cannot reach a diagnostic at this time until the inflammation in the brain is reduced and we can confirm that there are spontaneous movements by the patient, and her extremities move.

Christopher asked the surgeon to please not to deprive himself of resources for her. The daughters asked to see their mother. The Doctor ordered the nurse to let them in one by one, every fifteen minutes. Christopher asked Alain to ask on his behalf permission to stay with her all the time, but the Doctor said that not at this time, but, when she is responsive we will allow you to stay with her.

Later that day Alain, Camille, Chloe and Milam went to the tourist center and hired the interpreters for Christopher and Milam, so that Alain could take care of his daughter, then Christopher offered Chloe to stay in the hotel with Milam because she lived very far and had left her son with her husband and she would not go back home until her mother had recovered consciousness.

When Christopher's interpreter got to the hospital, Christopher asked Yanay to go home and rest for a while. He offered the translator to stay with him and that he would pay him well, that when Francesca's son-in-law was at the hospital, he could go home for a while and come back later.

Both sat in recliners and they watch the news. The interpreter would tell Christopher what was going on and then later, both of them fell asleep. At 4:00 in the afternoon a nurse arrived and woke Christopher up, who woke the interpreter up.

—Please ask the nurse what she wants.

—Your girlfriend is moving her fingers and complains of pain.

—Please ask the nurse to let me in for a few minutes before Francesca is given the pain killers again that will make her sleepy.

Christopher ran to get the sterilized clothes in order to go see Francesca.

Then the nurse asked him to get in the room as quiet as possible, when he got to the room he grabbed Francesca's hand and told her:

—My love, it's me Christopher, I am here. If you can listen to me, move your fingers. Then she moved her fingers.

He got so emotional that could not hold on anymore and started crying, once again. He grabbed her hand and kissed her hand. She was complaining and he asked her if she had a lot of pain, and she moved a finger up and down to let him know that she was in pain. Then the nurse called the intensive care unit doctor and with sign language asked Christopher to leave the room because the patient had to undergo evaluation, including questioning.

Christopher went to look for the interpreter and invited him to eat and have coffee. Then they both took a tour of the hospital and that way he could relax a little bit, while talking to each other.

Milam, Chloe and Milam's interpreter were already at the hotel, they had two king size beds for the three of them. They were talking and the interpreter offered Milam to take her to the Eiffel Tower the following morning so that she could see Paris a little. When the Interpreter was helping Chloe and Milam, Milam started throwing up, dizzy and unstable. Then, Chloe offered asking for a doctor at the hotel but Milam opposed to that suggestion.

—No, no, no. Do not worry for my symptoms. With me worrying about it, is more than enough.

The interpreter told Chloe:

—This girl is pregnant, I know because she is throwing up a lot and complains of pain in her chest.

Milam washed her mouth and lied on the bed and asked the interpreter if she could get some alcohol or something for nausea. Then, Chloe went to the front desk and ask for alcohol or something for nausea. He responded that he had some alcohol but for nausea would have to call a doctor. You can also go to a pharmacy and ask for it. Chloe took the alcohol to her and then told her:

—We are all women Milam, please let us know what is going on so that we can help you, please remember that we are not related by blood but from my observation we may soon become stepsisters.

Then Milam started crying and told them:

—It's that I am pregnant and my father has no clue!

—Why don't you tell him? Said Chloe.

—You don't know what you are talking about. My father has always been very strict with us, he doesn't smoke or drink, was always dedicated to my mother, to us and his business and my problem would be to him like another volcano erupting, I have to wait until your mother recuperates and then I will tell him.

The interpreter asked her:

—Have you considered the option to abort?

—No, I am a person of faith and don't believe in abortion, besides that in my country it is abolished by law and my father would be the first one to not forgive me, because we consider abortion to be a crime.

Then Chloe asked her:

—Who is the father of the baby?

—That is the worse part in this issue. I went to a night club with some friends and didn't have any alcoholic beverages but seems like someone put a drug in my soda and I don't remember anything after that. I woke up on the back seat of my car without panties, all my clothes were ripped off and my body was dirty and gluey because of the semen. I don't know if it was one or several men, all I can tell you is that I had pain in my vagina after that, for several days without telling anybody. You are the first to know about my problem. Please do not tell anybody. Can you imagine? I don't know if I was raped by a person with

AIDS or any other venereal decease. I don't even know the race of that person or if it was an extraterrestrial. I don't know anything.

Then the interpreter tried talking her into an abortion to be the best option.

—You don't know if you are bringing a baby to this world with a genetic illness or if the father was under the influence of a drug, or if you bring a baby with an abnormal syndrome to this world. In France, the abortion is free and normal and you don't need any kind of authorization. We can help you on that, please think about it now that you have the opportunity to do it.

After a while, thinking about it, Milam told them:

—As soon as I go back to my country, I will go see my doctor and ask him for a checkup and tests on any venereal deceases, but, by now I have to suffer in silence.

After having this conversation, they all took a shower, went to eat and went to bed.

Christopher was walking through the hospital halls. He went to see Francesca with the nurse's authorization. He also asked about the last Doctor's evaluation. The nurse then told him:

—The Doctor said that she was reacting very well and all tests came out better than the previous and so are her vital signs.

Christopher went to the room, sat by Francesca and taking her hand inclined his head to the bed. She was sedated, time passed by and he fell asleep until he felt someone touching his head and to his surprise it was Francesca's hand. He looked at her and asked her if she was feeling better and she did answer with a movement of her hand that meant yes.

—How happy I am! Thanks God, I can tell that you know

that I am here with you.

—Can you hear me talking? She made another sign with her hand that looked like more or less. Then, he softly touched the sole of her foot and she shrank the foot, which was a sign that her brain was working and she was able to walk, the reflexes of her body were working.

He stayed calmed and talking softly and in a low voice said:

—Dear, I love you very much. When I was informed of the accident I almost went crazy, my daughter wanted to accompany me and she is at the hotel with Chloe and an interpreter. Camille and Alain went home to sleep to be with their daughter, and tomorrow after they leave the girl at school are coming back. Do you really forgive me? He told her very close to her. then Francesca touched his head confirming his answer.

—My love, I will let you rest now but while you are falling sleep, I want to sing a song to you that reminds me of our love and he began singing some lyrics that made him think of the moment they met and fell in love.

The Boheme. Adapted by Christopher:

I talk of times which are unknown by persons under 20 years of age.

The Boheme, the Boheme, means we are happy;
When tired and happy we used to live a night of passion; And, when I was delineating the lines of your bust with my hands, I used to breath deeply and remember the days of our youth and crazy days; The Boheme, The Boheme,
Means you are beautiful; The Boheme, The Boheme.

—You see my love, how I also know about French Songs and know how to adapt them for you.

She was sleepy but smiled and touched his hands.

After that, also with sign language Francesca let him know that she had to rest and then he replied:

—I am not leaving this hospital until you have fully recovered but I will let you rest now.

Christopher came out of the room jumping like a child and went to a phone and called Milam, Camille, Yanay, Alain and his son, Richard. He was euphoric, he felt fulfilled because God was giving him back what he wanted the most, then he went back to the chapel and asked the Lord for forgiveness because of his blasphemies at the cabin. He asked the interpreter to go with him and talk to the nurse to let her know what had transpired at the recovery room. She promised to inform the Doctor of the whereabouts immediately. He explained to the nurse that since she was falling asleep he was going to sleep in an armchair for a while, then, the nurse offered to bring him a pillow and a throw, because she was aware of the fact that he spent the day in that armchair waiting for news. Then, he told the interpreter to go, rest and come back the following day after lunch, since he was having the family staying with him at the hospital the following morning and he would have help with the language.

The next morning, Milam, Chloe and the interpreter were at the hospital very early in the morning. They brought pastries for all. Chloe also brought Christopher a comb because she was tired to see him with the hairs out of place, she also brought him a tooth brush and toothpaste. He washed his face and teeth and waited for the doctors, because the girls insisted in him going to the hotel to rest because he could also get sick because of the circumstances. Chloe insisted and told her stepfather:

—You are both going to be sick and then neither you nor her can do anything for the other.

—Dad, Chloe is right, said Milam. I also wanted to tell you that the interpreter wants to take me to the Eiffel Tower this afternoon. Would it bother you if I go? She is telling me that I am leaving and I have not seen Paris.

Then, when the doctors arrived to talk to the relatives, all of the relatives were there. They were told that if the recovery kept going as well as it was happening, she would be transferred to a regular room in three days to start the recovery process and if she didn't have any side effects she could go home and come to the hospital for therapy.

Three days after that, as expected, she was transferred to a private room, the enormous bandage was removed from her head and they left a very small bandage where necessary, she was not speaking a lot but her eyes were open. Christopher asked the family to bring him cloth since he was going to shower in the bathroom at the room and did not intend to leave the hospital until she was discharged. Milam was leaving in a couple of days and she asked her father to let her stay that night with Francesca, that he could go to the hotel with Chloe to rest and then she could at least spend a night with Francesca before leaving to the United States. Francesca heard Milam talking to her father and in a low voice near his ear told him:

—Accept her offer, I also want to spend several hours with her alone to get to know her better.

Finally, he left to the hotel with Chloe. When Francesca and Milam were alone, accompanied only by the interpreter, Milam asked the Interpreter to help her communicate with Francesca and that she needed her to explain her problem to Francesca in detail.

—Francesca, if I explain to you a delicate problem I have, would it make you feel bad? I don't want you to get emotional if you are not in a condition to go through that stage, but I need your help and understanding as a woman and also as my future mother, as you are. I need you to talk to my father. I am going to ask Eugene, my interpreter, to explain my situation to you, Eugene and Chloe know what it's going on, but, please don't tell my father until I have left France, and when you feel a little bit better. He is a very good person, but sometimes he gets very mad over certain circumstances and is too conservative for certain things.

Francesca accepted and after having heard what the problem was, then she told Milam:

—The most important thing here is for you to worry about your mental health, you have gone through a rape and you need to have a medical checkup done, you must also see a psychologist because if you have a child you need to get out of the trauma that you have suffered, so that you can see the child as a gift and not as a result of a bad experience. (She told her in a soft warm voice to demonstrate her interest in the matter). Then, continued...

—Don't worry so much about your dad, sooner or later he will have to understand, I promise I will talk to him and make him understand that this happens every day everywhere in the world and unfortunately it happened to you. This is the time for him to demonstrate how he cares for you and his love for you and help you heal the suffering you have gone through. Whenever you feel bad you can count on me because I will dedicate all the time to help you receive that child that is getting to your life with love and happiness.

—Francesca, you are really a beautiful person, I can understand why my father fell in love with you and got desperate when he thought that he had lost you.

—Francesca, I promise, I will be back soon to help you

with your recovery. Then, Francesca responded…

—Believe me, I will not lose my old man ever, he is mine since the first time he stole a kiss from me and I kissed him for the first time.

The nurse announced another visit saying.

—But, try to speak as little as possible so that you don't lose strength. Only, 30 minutes per visit and then you have to rest.

Yanay arrived with her brother, who was an extremely good looking guy, tall, with defined muscles, brunette and with a lot of charm. When he entered the room he took Francesca's hand and gave her a kiss and told her.

—I am very happy to see you have recovered, Yanay kept me informed of the whereabouts of your illness, my sister has suffered like if it would have been her own mother.

—Francesca replied that she knew and that she loved his sister like a daughter.

Yanay's brother whose name was Pierre was happy to see her in a good mood and expressed it:

—I am so happy to find you in a good mood Francesca! And, where is your American Guy? Because I understand that he has been with you all the time.

—Pierre, we have just made him leave to rest but he left this beauty, his daughter, Milam, who is the daughter of the man I love.

Pierre had noticed Milam and her beauty since he entered the room.

—Your words are perfect, she is a beauty, he responded.

Then Milam after hearing the translation of his words, smiled and looked at him for the first time and said "Thank you". Then she looked down but thinking that he was also a masculine beauty, and thought; how sad to be under these circumstances, if not, I would have hit back at him.

When the nurse asked the group to retire from the room. Then they all went to the waiting room and since Pierre didn't want to leave so soon, he invited the three women to have ice cream across the street from the hospital. Yanay, with her big mouth told him:

—Pierre, I thought you were in a hurry. What made you change your mind?

—Oh, Yanay! You are always getting involved. Why are you like this?

The interpreter told him not to worry that she was not translating this last conversation. Milam asked the Interpreter.

—What are you talking about?

Then, Eugene said:

—Don't worry. It has nothing to do with you. Then Milam said: I have to learn French. Then Pierre asked:

—What is she saying? When he knew what she said he replied:

—She has to learn French and I have to learn English.

They went to the ice cream shop and tears came out of Milam's eyes. Yanay asked her what was happening and Milam said:

—I just remembered that my father and my mother fell in love in an ice cream shop.

As they were parting, Pierre took her hand and she looked at his eyes for a while. She then put her sight down and said bye because she had to return to the hospital to stay with Francesca. When they got to the hospital room Milam and Eugene lied down in the sofa bed because Francesca was totally asleep.

When Yanay and Pierre left the ice cream shop, Yanay told her brother the situation Milam was going through at that time and recommended him to forget about her because she was going to have a child of another man and that was a problem. Pierre answered:

—If she recovers emotionally from this problem, I don't mind marrying her.

Yanay was surprised and replied:

—Hey, don't you think that it's too soon to be in love with her?

—And what about the girlfriend you spoke about, continued Yanay. What are you going to do with her?

—If this American Girl accepts me, I will get rid of the other, without a doubt.

—Wow. Here is another one, said Yanay. First Francesca with her prince and what about you? Have you found your Princess?

—Maybe, said Pierre.

Christopher arrived with Chloe to the hospital the next morning. He brought Francesca a beautiful flower bouquet and a teddy bear that bought at the hotel. He asked his daughter to go to the hotel and rest and later visit some of Paris' touristic places because she was leaving the following day. She agreed. When Milam was leaving, a man accompanied by his family was entering the room. Christopher recognized the man immediately and knew that it was Francesca's brother, but besides that, he felt uncomfortable thinking about that horrible day and felt some sort of pressure on his neck, up to a point that he let him passed by until he got out of the shock.

Finally, Christopher went back into the room where Francesca was with her brother, his wife and their son. Francesca introduced them:

—Christopher, this is my brother.

—Christopher said, my pleasure, met his wife and asked

how they were doing. Some minutes after that, his brother-in-law approached Christopher and said:

—I finally met my American brother-in-law, I never imagined having an American brother-in-law, as much as I like them!

—Alexander, watch your language, Francesca told her brother in French. I will not translate your lack of courtesy with Americans , he has in one occasion been very explicit to Chloe's husband about this issue. I am not going to repeat what you said. -OK!

—What are you talking about the Americans? Asked Christopher.

—My brother was telling me, that you are very nice people.

—Thank you!

They spent several hours together at the hospital when the doctor arrived and asked the group to wait outside. Christopher had the courtesy of inviting them to the cafeteria downstairs and to have whatever they pleased. Then they all went back to the waiting room to talk to the doctor. They were all together when Christopher's Interpreter arrived. Francesca was going to have a complete evaluation and tests, such as Scan, MRI, Electro Cardiogram, blood tests and a Psychological Evaluation. If all came back normal she was going home within 48-72 hours. Under absolute bed rest for approximately 30 days, with a follow-up visit with her primary care physician in two weeks.

Forty-eight hours had passed and all results came back normal, then Christopher took her to the hotel suite with him. Chloe stayed with them for a few days and then went back to her husband and child. Christopher gave Chloe an envelope and asked her not to open the envelope until she got home to her husband, that he would talk to them later. Francesca asked him what had he given Chloe and he responded: I gave her a check because they were not very well off and there is an economic crisis. He estimated that she needed the money and Chloe was a great kid. He saw her the same as Milam. Francesca then told him:

—Christopher, since I have met you, you have spent a lot of money. You are a very good-hearted person, but, where are you heading?

—I don't want you to worry about expenses, I know when to stop.

—I want to go to my apartment. I feel better taking care of my business.

—Please, do not insist. I wish I could take you home with me for a vacation, but, we have to wait until the doctors let you travel.

—You have to take care of your business, Francesca replied.

—I am working from here through my computer. I have not stopped working, but, let me tell you I spoke to Alain long time ago and an elevator is being installed in your place and the stairs are being remodeled in a few days. It's a miracle that Yanay has not told you. That way you can go to your apartment from the business. I don't want you to use those stairs ever.

—More expenses. You are crazy. Stop spending money, I will not use the stairs at all. I will remain in the apartment until you come back.

—All right! Do you want to be my wife?

—Of course. I do.

—I am not a "macho man", but I want you to know that I am the head of the family not the last in line and I make the decisions in this family.

CHAPTER XV
FRANCESCA'S RE-BIRTH

Fourteen days had elapsed since the last conversation and they were on their way to the doctor's office to find out about the results of the last tests from the Hospital and also to make sure that she was already discharged to have a normal way of life. The doctor told them that all tests came out normal and then tried some tests on her body to determine if her brain was functioning and no side effects were found. Then, Christopher asked Francesca to translate for him in some questions he had.

—Doctor, please let me know if she can travel. Can she do the chores of a housewife? Can she have sex?

—She can do several things but little by little in her recovery stage but she has to go slowly, the Doctor replied to his questions. I want to see her in a couple of weeks to have the tests done again. My assistant will now give you the orders for the tests and schedule the dates with the different departments. –Francesca was translating for both of them.

On the way out Christopher asked the Doctor again (Francesca translating again):

—Can I have sexual intimacy with my wife? Please let me know. May I or not?

—I told you little by little according to how she feels and her tolerance.

When they were leaving the office, the Doctor was commenting with his assistant:

—What is this old man talking about?

Francesca heard the doctor's comment and in French:

—Doctor, you would be surprised. My husband's testosterone is as high as that one of a 45 year old man and I am also high in Hormones.

The Doctor did not respond. Christopher asked the taxi driver to take them to her apartment. She was surprised and he noticed and told her there was a surprise waiting for her. He called Yanay at the business and told her:

—Put a sign on the door stating that we are closed for the day, we are already on our way.

—Yes, your majesty. It's all ready. Am I leaving?

—No Yanay, don't leave.

When they arrived Francesca noticed that the door was closed and mentioned it to Christopher.

—You see. That's why I have to take care of my business, do you think that there is logic for the business to be closed at this time? Wait till I see Yanay, we will have a long conversation.

Francesca didn't have the key to the business with her and got very nervous but Christopher calmed her down:

—Be quiet, Yanay is inside.

She felt a little bit more calmed. Yanay opened the door for her with tears running down her face.

—Oh, my queen. I need you so much! Francesca responded to her:

—That's why I cannot call your attention.

She looked down and noticed that the rug was full of rose petals, her favorite. She observed that the petals were all the way to the stairs and next to the stairs. The stairs were remodeled with wooden rails varnished the same as the steps. Nothing like the old stairs and there was an elevator that couldn't be seen from the business, where a closet used to be. The elevator was made of a very light green crystal and was very pretty, the color of her eyes, with capacity for only one person. Then, Francesca's eyes got watery and told him:

—Oh, my beloved American King! You are so good to

me!; This is like living a fairy tale, you have me in an unlimited flow of attentions and demonstrations of love. I never imagined that God had destined so much happiness and love at the end of my life. Who could have told me that at my 60 years of age I was going to find happiness and was going to fall in love again. How can I not fall in love with you?

Yanay jumped to her statements and said:

—Christopher, I told you that I shouldn't be here today. I joke a lot but this is your moment.

—No Yanay, we are all going to celebrate Francesca's recovery and if you wish you can leave and have the rest of the day off. You deserve that and more.

Francesca boarded the elevator and Christopher and Yanay used the stairs. When she got to the apartment, she couldn't believe what she was looking at and all she could say was:

—Oh… but, what have you done? It's all so beautiful! You have changed all of my furniture and decorations, but, what did you do with my furniture?

—I gave them all to Camille, he responded.

—Well, she always liked my furniture.

—But, don't you like this new furniture? —asked Christopher.

—It's all beautiful, responded Francesca. Don't you think that the bed is too high? I can't not reach up there; (the bed was also full of rose petals).

—Don't worry love, the bed has remote control, goes up and down and vibrates.

—Like the rapid train?

—A little bit faster.

She continued her tour through the apartment and noticed that he had used one of the balconies to make the apartment bigger. She used to have that section for cloth and accessories, instead of that there was a small room with a desk and a computer for Christopher, so that he could work from her apartment. On top of the center table there was a big arrangement of flowers and a dish full of strawberries covered with chocolate, caviar and a cold bottle of champagne. Francesca hesitated and finally told him:

—No, not yet, remember little by little and slowly and if you decide to give me a bath in Champagne, please make sure it's not cold.

—No, I will not use or bathe you with it.

Then, Yanay told them:

—Do you bathe in Champagne? That is too expensive. Since when do you bathe in it?

Francesca told her not to ask questions that are so direct; that the Champagne is a very private matter between the two of them, she added.

In the hall on the way to the bathroom there was a big picture frame showing the pictures of all the places they had visited together. In the center of that picture there was a bigger picture of a King and a Queen, that had both their faces.

—Christopher, who did all this job?

—I asked Alain to hire a decorator that works for the hotel and she took care of all of these details. I am as surprised as you, because I couldn't come to see what was going on. Yanay arranged the flowers, and bought the champagne and the strawberries covered with chocolate. We will now drink to celebrate this rebirth. After the Champagne he asked Yanay to please leave.

—Go get your policeman that I will stay with my queen.

Yanay left. Christopher went to the computer and put

a CD to play a song by Lionel Richie "Hello", and then told Francesca:

—Can you dance a little and slowly with me?

—Yes, she repeated after him, a little and slowly.

They started to dance very slowly and he started kissing her, first in the mouth and then in the neck. Then, he opened her blouse and took her bra off and Francesca jumped and told him:

—Hey! Be careful, little by little, my love.

He continued touching her breasts and kissing her and she kept complaining:

—Hey...Hey...! Slowly, only a little.

He paid no attention and kept taking the rest of her cloth off. Then she let her hand reach the zipper of his pants and touched it softly. Then he told her:

—Hey! is this what you call a little?

She took all of his cloth off asking him, please don't overdo it, because she had to be careful, but, at the same time she said.

—Just a little, a little, my love. Then he turned her back to him and brought her body very close to his. With his right hand he was touching her right breast and with the left hand he was touching the most private zone of a woman's body.

In a very low voice she asked him.

—My love, why don't we go to bed? I am getting weak and that way I don't get that tired. So they did. They spent all afternoon in the apartment and later on ordered Chinese Food for them and for Camille, her husband and her granddaughter that had already arrived on time to eat. The girl almost breaks the elevator going up and down, until Camille noticed and asked her to stop.

—Baby, you are going to break your Grandma's elevator.

You could tell that there was more rap port between Camille and her husband, the way they looked at each other showed more confidence, Camille with the worry for her mother's accident had lost ten pounds. She had dyed her hair a very bright reddish that contrasted with her eyes. Francesca was observing her and told Christopher:

—My love, it seems like your magic wand worked for this couple. When the family left, Francesca told Christopher:

—Love. I have something very serious to tell you.

—Don't scare me, does it have to do with you?

—It's not me, don't worry, but, please forgive me for having kept this to myself until today. I beg you to stay calmed and listen to me first and then express yourself. I couldn't tell you before because I was not strong enough to tell you something that would make you suffer.

—Why suffering?

—I asked you to listen to me first.

—OK, Francesca, let's get to it already, not more advances, I am impatient.

—Your daughter has recently had an accident.

—What kind of accident?

—Please, my love, let me finish, the night that Milam stayed with me at the hospital asked me to talk to you about her incident, but to wait until I was stronger and she was already gone. She went to a night club after work with the young people at her office, apparently someone put a drug in her soda without her noticing. She then disappeared from the group and woke up on the back seat of her car, without the panty, with her cloth ripped, wet and raped.

—Who was the son of a bitch that hurt my daughter?

—She doesn't know. She was not accompanied by any man, she doesn't even remember how she ended up separated from her friends. It could have been anybody and maybe more than one.

—I have to call Milam right now. His face was already different and tense and you could tell that his chest was tight.

Francesca got scared and worried and told him:

—Christopher, please do it for me, I am still weak and you are making me nervous. Call her tomorrow and please let me finish. Milam is also very delicate under psychological treatment. There is something else, you are going to be a grandfather of your first grandson by Milam. What I am telling you is very strong, but receive this child as a gift from God.

Francesca continued explaining:

—If all of the medical and psychological results come out normal, that baby is going to be a blessing in our lives. I hope it is a boy and inherits your tantrums and your sweetness.

—You are asking me to accept a grandchild from my daughter without knowing who the father is. My wife went to me in front of the priest being a virgin.

—Yes, my love, but these are different times we are living and your daughter is 32 years old. She has a career, takes care of your business and you have to look at this like an accident. I am sure that if your wife would have been here she would have been supporting her daughter. What if she would have been killed? Thank God for having your daughter alive. With or without your consent I will support her, Christopher.

He was walking the apartment from one place to the other until he threw himself in an armed chair, crying and groaning like a child. Francesca didn't know what to do to comfort him. She finally asked him that if calling his daughter would make him feel better to go ahead and do it.

—Francesca, this is not the first time that I cry and groan like this, I also got like this when I lost my parents, my 12-year old child and my wife and when I thought you were dying, in which occasion I cried in silence, but it hurt the same. The same way we sleep together and live together in the good and bad times, I am crying here now.

He called his daughter when he was calmed and told her:

—My kid, I love you under any circumstances. Francesca told me that we are going to have a grandchild product of an accident in your life. Look at it from that perspective. What really hurts me is that you did not tell me first.

—I didn't tell anybody. I told the woman you love and that occupies a very important place in our lives. Almost like a mother. She is an angel that God brought into our lives. If it serves to make you feel better, let me tell you that all of the medical results are normal. If you accept me and accept my child, I will not need psychological or medical assistance, all I need is my Father.

Short separation

Christopher was obligated to separate from Francesca for a short period of time. He had to go back to the United States for business matters. When he left, he told Francesca that he would use his trip to obtain her legal entrance to the United States. He wanted to establish her in his country once she was completely recovered. He wanted to prepare conditions for her arrival in his house, in the Cabin and in his business.

He had abandoned his business for over a month and he was thinking that "when the cat is away the mice are at play". His son was always a very responsible man but was lacking the experience he had learned in the business world. He remembered that the economy was in crisis and the sales had gone down, as his son had told him. That is why he had to go back in person and "manage the business," including a cut in expenses until the economy got better. Francesca had commented that she was also having loses because of the crisis in the economy and she called his attention to the following:

—That is why I have told you several times not to spend so much money, please remember that we are of age and in approximately 15 years we would have to retire for good.

—I am going over there and I don't know when I will be back, it might take me 15 or 30 days, but maybe a little bit longer. I want to hire the services of an immigration attorney. I am going to claim you as an Investor that is faster than claiming a relative. I don't intend to open a business for you, I want you with me in my business so that we can leave on a trip whenever we want. On top of that, I want to hire a maid to help you with the chores of the house.

—No, my love, it's Francesca's answer. I have Yanay and will not incur in any more expenses. In the worst case scenario, I will bring Yanay to live with me until you come back.

Christopher left for the United States and as soon as he got home, he called Milam to come to his house to have dinner with him. He was going to meet with Richard the following day to go over business matters. He wanted to see his daughter first and have a conversation with her.

Milam, immediately left to his dad's house, they hugged, kissed and she started crying, because she was extremely sensitive because of her maternity. Christopher was very worried because of the fact that they didn't know who the father of the child was or if the child will inherit congener illnesses. Milam told her dad:

—Dad, all of the lab results came back normal, the child is not coming with Aids or any other venereal decease. When I am four months pregnant they will give me a test to see if the child is normal, if not, then they will probably recommend abortion. Christopher responded:

—God forbid us for having to go through an abortion when you are already four-months pregnant. But, please let me know about your plans as a single mother. Are you going to keep practicing in your career?

—Of course, I will keep my practice and I can leave the baby with one of my maids and go to work. I will not look for a stranger but, I can leave the child in your home.

—Do you have a person?

—No Dad, I am not in the mood.

—Haven't you thought of the need of a father for the child?

—No, I am happy with your last name.

—You have to think about this, and later on, you might have a change of mind.

—When he went to his business, he hugged his son and asked for an emergency meeting, where he spoke to all of his employees and expressed the critical economic times the country was going through. He offered the following solutions:

—I have no other alternative but to take action in order for us not having to give layoffs to our people. We all have needs and if there are employees who cannot deal with the cuts I need to make, can go and find a job somewhere else. At this moment, I need to cut the weekly hours from 40 to 32. There will not be any over time and no annual bonuses until further notice. I am trying to get an HMO Insurance Plan instead of the PPO Health Plan, which is more expensive. But I will not stop providing medical insurance coverage. From now on, we cannot lose a single client, we have to treat clients like kings, no matter what the client's behavior is.

—The information I gave you today will be spread throughout all branches of this business. The other employees will receive a letter explaining all of these changes.

The first action Christopher carried away was Francesca's immigration issues and those of her family. Including, permit exceptions given to the Europeans to come to the United States for a period of two years, coming to the country and leaving during certain periods of time. This authorization or permit is called "ESTA".

He explained all this to Francesca in a telephone conversation.

—I already applied for your visa and also Camille's, Alain and the child. I should have the visas in 72 hours, so arrange for appointments with your doctors to obtain the discharge. Also, organize your pending business matters with Yanay. I want you here with me as soon as possible. Love at a distance is not for me and if we have to get married later, we will start to expedite those papers.

—Yes, sir. I already know that from now on you take the decisions in the family, "you are the head of the family not the last one". Those words are very fixed in my mind, I know I cannot decide anything, but, under one condition, that the welcome back has to be with lots of rose petals, cold and warm champagne, strawberries with chocolate and a very hard drill.

—Francesca, who are you doing business with in France?

—I have enough with my assistant, Yanay, she doesn't even let me look at the stairs; elevator all the time, because she says that her duty is to look after me. Believe it or not I have been taking note in a calendar of these 40 days that have elapsed. I feel very sad and anxious, I cannot sleep well. Or, I go to you or you have to come back to me. I will be there in seven days, my passport is ready and I have been discharged by all doctors.

—Camille is coming here in a few days, she already has money for the tickets, money that you gave them when you invited them. You will have your house full of French people.

—How nice!

—I am dying to see your daughter, hug her and talk to her about her expectancy. She is almost four months pregnant and I want to be with her the day they give her a test. Yanay had arranged for Milam to have a conversation with her brother Pierre, since he is driving her crazy, but, no progress by Milam's side. Pierre was getting desperate because he didn't want to lose her and asked help from a friend that owned a business in the United States and the friend claimed him as an investor and obtained a special permit for a visit to the United States.

Pierre finally arrived in Maryland without notice. He booked at a Holiday Inn Hotel that was close to Milam's business.

When Milam got out of bed, the day was cloudy and rainy, she woke up thinking about her expectancy and she told herself that it is a beautiful feeling to expect a child and I only live for him, but, her life as a woman had stopped. I cannot feel anything. I am dead inside. When is this horrible feeling going to end? She kept asking herself.

Pierre woke up under the same sky and very early went directly to Milam's business to wait for her to pass by, he waited inside the building by the elevator, he thought that sooner or later she would show up to go to work and would take the elevator. Before leaving France he took English Classes for a month with a good professor, practicing English. When Milam was approaching, he followed her and when was passing by him, he told her:

—This beautiful blonde has the cutest belly ever!

She noticed that it was not perfect English what she heard and turned to look at the person. She did not recognize him and asked herself.

—Who is that? and kept walking. Then he told her:

—Milam, it's me, Pierre, Yanay's brother.

She made a sudden stop and asked him:

—What are you doing here?

—I have been following your perfume from France, because I want to marry you.

—Are you not aware of my situation and pregnancy?

—Talk slowly so that I can understand what you are saying? Please don't work today, spend one day with me so that I can explain, what I want from you.

—I have appointments and clients waiting for me.

—You can call in sick or tell them that you have problems with your car.

—You are very persistent and impulsive (she was thinking: "I like him").

—Pierre said that he had a fancy translator, since he is a computer programmer.

She answered:

—I also have a translation equipment in my briefcase to communicate with my foreign clients.

They sat at a nearby cafeteria and asked for sodas and sandwiches, then she approached him:

—Be honest. What is it that you want from me?

—I am only looking for love. I fell in love with your looks

and I would love to be the owner of your person and also of the person you carry inside you.

—Have you measured the extent of your words?

—At least, I have repeated it a million of times to be able to tell you.

—What is your goal? Get a visa and then a green card or live by my monetary standards.

—I am not interested in your money or the green card. If you want, you can leave with me and live in France with a computer programmer.

—Pierre, I have to go to work. Can't stay any longer. This is my address, I live with my father. I am inviting you to dinner in my house tonight.

He approached her and tried kissing her in the cheek, but she stepped backwards, extended her hand and told him:

—I'll see you tonight.

Immediately after that, he called her dad's business and got the address. He asked if Christopher was at work and someone confirmed that he was at the business. Then, hung up very fast and took a taxi. He showed up at the business and asked to see Christopher. When he saw him Pierre reminded Christopher that he was Yanay's brother, then, they hugged and Christopher told him:

—Good to see you, Yanay has spoken a lot about you and I am immensely grateful to her. What are you doing here?

—I have come to see you.

—That's fine. What can I do for you?

—I know it is difficult for you to understand what I have to say and it is difficult for me too, but, I love your daughter.

—Where did you meet my daughter?

—I met her at the hospital when Francesca was

hospitalized, I got to see her with my sister the night after when she left France. Milam has bewitched me, I cannot stop thinking about her and I am even taking English lessons to tell her how I feel about her. I am invited to have dinner with you at your house and I want you to consent in my request to marry her and take her child as mine. I don't care about your wealth or the green card.

—All right. Do I see you tonight or do you wish to stay here with me?

—No, thank you. I have to go. A friend of mine who owns a computer shop is just about to pick me up, because I am a computer programmer and my friend claimed me with a business visa.

—Good. The computers are always giving us problems here.

Dinner time came, she asked him to be there at 7:00 o'clock sharp and it was 7:15 and he had not shown up and she was impatient. Her father was observing her and her body language.

—Why is not the table set?

—I asked the maid to set the table later.

—I am not a picture hung in the wall. Please ask the maid to set the table.

—Dad. Please wait a few minutes. I invited someone to dinner.

—Who is it? A girlfriend of yours?

—No, dad. I invited a male friend.

—Oh…! And, who is that friend?

—Pierre, Yanay's brother.

—Oh…! What is he doing here and how did you get in contact with him?

—No, Dad. He looked for me and contacted me and I invited him to dinner here so I didn't have to meet him somewhere else.

—Well, explain?

—I don't know dad and I am not in a situation to maintain a relationship.

—Daughter, do you like him?

—I don't know Dad.

—I asked you a question, please respond.

—He is very attractive and seems to be smart and a hard working person.

—What is he looking for? You are beautiful, smart and a good girl, but, do you know if he is interested in some- thing else?

—I have already asked him about that and he is only interested in me. At that precise moment they heard the door bell and the maid went to get the door, as usual.

—Wait Guadalupe. I will get the door. The maid responded:

—What a surprise! My lady is interested in getting the door for the visitor. I also had her in the kitchen ordering around. Seems like "this egg is asking for salt". Don't you agree Mr. Christopher?

—I agree with you, Guadalupe.

When Milam was walking towards the door the father observed that her steps looked insecure and her hands were trembling. Christopher then had this thought "maybe this is another angel that fell from the sky for us".

She finally opened the door for him and when Pierre saw her he stepped on the wrong place by the entrance, she had to hold him and a big bunch of red roses he brought her, almost fell on the floor.

—I am sorry, my friend got lost and I am late.

—Come in!

He was looking at the sculptures, the columns made of

Italian Marble and a huge Persian Rug that would need six men to carry. He asked for Christopher and the maid ran to set the table the way Milam had instructed. On the way to the kitchen the maid was asking herself, who needs two forks and two knives to eat. Pierre instead of giving her the bunch of roses, gave them to the father.

Christopher then told him:

—No, not to me. Give them to her.

—I am sorry! I am nervous.

—Milam these roses are for you.

She took them:

—Thank you! I always figured they were mine.

—Pierre, come with us outside to the terrace before dinner. Said Christopher.

The maid brought Champagne and cheese cuts. Milam and Christopher asked for Yanay and Francesca and her family. Then Christopher wanted to conduct the conversation to make it easier for them.

—Milam. I know Pierre is here to ask me for permission to have a relationship with you.

—How do you know that?

—Let me tell you. He went to see me at the business and we had a conversation regarding this matter.

Right before entering into the dining room, Christopher started giving Pierre a speech, as follows:

Christopher told them that women were almost extinct. That he liked women that wanted to be princesses, with good manners, honest and with high moral qualities and men that are gentlemen to the women. The women that struggle to be more of a woman and that would not compete with men. With women's liberation, many women wanted to do the same things men do: visit bars to have drinks and practice free love, who are subject to abuse by men, and we cannot distinguish between a lady and a gentleman. They dress in pants, shirts, a wide belt and boots. That way of life confuses them.

I like women who do not want to turn into men. That study in Universities and obtain a certificate, women that don't look at a man because of his wealth, but a man to love and make her happy. That was the life that Milam's mother and I lived and that is the life that I want for Francesca and for my daughter. These are the rules to follow and to accept you as a candidate for my daughter.

After listening to Christopher, Pierre replied to him:

—Sir, I didn't come so far to ask for a relationship with your daughter and waste your time. I have left many pretty women in France and very well off, but, they do not fulfill me. Milam has me under a spell since the day I met her. The way you have lived as a conservative man, which you are, is what I want to live with your daughter. Then, they heard a bell to let them know that the table was ready.

—Guadalupe is calling, but, it was Milam who took care of the table and the dinner, very unusual for her.

—Can you think of anything better to say, dad?

—You can arrange the flowers in a bud base so that we can sit and eat.

They were all quiet at the table and meditating all that was previously said.

Guadalupe kept thinking: Either the food was good or Pierre was hungry. He ate it all and kept saying that the menu chosen was great. After dinner, she served Christopher his coffee and apple pie and ice cream to the younger couple. After dessert they stayed having a conversation at the table. Christopher told Pierre that he knew he was in the United States as a tourist but

—What are your immediate plans? Do you plan to

stay in the United States or do you want to go back to France? Pierre responded:

—I am French and feel more comfortable in France and my career is established over there, the language is another issue. It is like a new beginning, but, if Milam accepts my offer and does not want to live in France I would have to determine what makes us both happy.

Christopher said:

—I would never accept to have my daughter taken away from me. I am bringing Francesca and her family to the United States, little by little. If you want, I will also have Yanay come here and stay with us. Pierre told him:

—I don't want to separate this family. My intentions are to love her and for her to love me. If here, here will be.

—What do you think about this Milam?

Milam was astonished to see how they were trying to manage her life and told them:

—What beautiful plans you both make for me. I am surprised to see how you two plan my future, like if I was a decoration or a picture in the wall. I am 32 years old and have a child coming, don't you feel that I am mature enough to decide my life. Pierre responded to her statements:

—The first thing I told you was that your child would become my child, I would adopt him and give him my name and I am willing to take care of his upbringing in a home with a mother and a father.

—My mother's name is Angela. If a girl. How would you name her?- asked Pierre.

—I made a promise at the Hospital's Chapel in front of Virgin Mary, that if it was a girl and was healthy I would name her Marie because of my prayers to the Virgin.

—Wouldn't you like better naming her Maria de los Angeles?

—I don't know. I would also like to name her with my mother's name after Marie, but, I don't think it sounds good. What do you think dad?

—I don't want to give an opinion. You two have not even kissed yet and you are already making plans with the name of the child. Make plans first and then talk about other things later. First, Pierre has to file his papers with immigration which takes time, is not a matter of a day. He has to go back to France and you will separate again. That would be the perfect time to decide what you really want.

—I am sorry, Christopher, what if she wants to go back to France with me while I obtain the papers. We'll marry before I leave and I'll take her with me until we can come back.

—You said that you were not here to interfere in our lives. Don't even think about it, she is not going anywhere under her circumstances. I don't like how you are making decisions, you and I are going to have some problems.

Milam then added to her dad's words—Pierre, I want my son to be born in the United States. Please let's get to know each other during your stay.

CHAPTER XVI
FRANCESCA'S ARRIVAL

Francesca arrived in the United States. Christopher picked her up at the airport with his son Richard and took a sign that read "Welcome to the United States" and also a bunch of flowers. Milam hugged her and told her how beautiful she looked out of that hospital.

—My father was right.

Richard looked at her jealous, thinking about his mother. Christopher noticed and asked him:

—You are not going to say hello to the lady?

Christopher was the translator from Spanish to English so that Richard and Francesca were able to communicate.

—Yes, of course. How are you, madam?

—I feel good, thank you and let me tell you that you look a lot like your father.

He responded with a simple:

—Thank you.

Christopher went with her to get the baggage and all went from the airport directly to Christopher's house.

When they arrived Francesca stood up in front of the house and said:

—What a beautiful house. It looks like a castle!

—Wait until you look inside.

When she entered the house she observed all of the furniture, the decorations and a picture of his wife. She took the flowers that he had taken to the airport for her, asked him for a vase and put the flowers under his wife's picture. Then, Richard told her:

—Thank you, madam, for such a nice gesture, may I kiss you in the cheek?

—Of course! I was missing that kiss. You will soon be

like a son to me.

Richard felt uncomfortable for the attitude he had at the airport. Francesca asked Christopher to take her outside to look at the surroundings of the house, because she felt tense after having spent so many hours on the plane.

—Do you want to eat or drink something?

—I want an American coffee just like you made me get used to in France.

—Don't tell me? I bought café latte specially for you and you ask me for American coffee. It's true that you never know what to get a woman.

—That's fine, I'll have a French Coffee.

—Are we having dinner here Dad?

—Yes Milam, let's reunite all the family in tonight's dinner.

—Can I invite Pierre Dad?

—Remember that I didn't like his suggestion of getting married and taking you to France, if you invite him, ask him not to mention that issue.

—I will never leave you Dad. Not because of Pierre or anyone else, but you have to give me an opportunity.

—What are you talking about Pierre? —asked Francesca.

—Yanay's brother.

—How is this happening? She hasn't said anything to me but let me tell you that I have a good opinion about that kid. Then, Richard asked:

—Who is Pierre?

—It is the man that went to see me at the business yesterday.

—The brunette guy with the tight pullover that sees himself as a strong guy.

—Hey brother, he doesn't see himself as a strong guy, he is.

—Now we are done. The French stepmother and brother-in-law. Looks like it's dangerous for this family to visit France.

—Richard please don't call me Stepmother. Call me Francesca or my dad's girlfriend. I am very honest. Ask your dad.

—I didn't want to make you feel bad.

—I am not upset. Just letting you know because that name sounds very distant and I want to love his children like I love my daughters.

—Thank you, madam. Not madam, Francesca.

Milam ran to the phone to invite Pierre for dinner.

—If you want, I need you to be here in a couple of hours. Francesca arrived from France and we are going to have a family dinner.

—I won't miss that dinner for anything in this world. Not the dinner or you.

—Pierre please, wear a normal shirt, not a pullover.

At dinner time that night they all gathered and talked like family. Pierre was very talkative because Francesca served as interpreter for him. Richard said bye to everybody and left. Milam accompanied Pierre to the door. The father was looking at them from a distance and saw how they closed the door and went outside into the garden. Francesca asked him if he wanted to go or lie down instead, but he responded:

—Not yet. I watch a series every night and it is almost over.

Christopher kept looking at the front entrance and Milam wouldn't come back. Then Francesca asked him:

—Are you waiting for somebody else?

—No. The thing is that Milam has not come back.

She is still outside.

—Your daughter is not a child. You are afraid of someone taking her away from you, because "cats don't like to be scratched".

They watched the series for approximately 20 minutes when Milam came back and was smiling. Christopher asked his maid to leave and rest as he was going to do the same. Francesca inquired about the maid:

—Have this lady that works here in the house as maid been working for a long time for you?

—Since she was born. Guadalupe's mother and her had no place to stay and no family. As a result, my mother asked them to come here to stay with us. She was brought up with us and has lived with us ever since.

—How nice!

When they got to the room she sat on top of the bed and told him that the mattress felt good and the room and the bathroom were very pretty. He asked her to get comfortable. Then she went to the bathroom and to the vanity and wore a transparent desaville. He looked at her and whistled and complemented her. He was sitting in the bed in his under ware waiting for her. She sat on top of his legs and asked him:

—How do I look my love?

—Beautiful, enchanting as always.

She took his head and bringing his ear close to her, told him:

—Tell me one of those pretty phrases you used to tell me in France.

—You are like the French Language. I don't understand it but I like it a lot.

—Another one, my love.

—My lips have an appointment of love with yours. Is that possible?

—Yes love! Then she pushed him against the bed. Let's stop the running around, we haven't been together in months.

They started kissing, he bit her neck on the back softly and she felt something different, sensual. He asked her what number she would like for the lottery and she responded very curious:

—Why that question?

—Because I believe we should play a game of two numbers.

—How do play that game?

—I will show you in bed.

When they finished playing he asked her if she liked the game. Her response was:

—I loved it, I won the Lotto!

—This is just a snack, right?

—If you agree, I am ready for dinner.

Two hours elapsed until they fell asleep. It was a very intense day and full of emotions. When they woke up, Guadalupe had the breakfast ready with three servings. Milam kissed them both and left.

—I have an appointment and I am running late.

—Daughter, please drive carefully, you are pregnant.

—By the way dad, please excuse me but don't wait for me for dinner. Francesca, enjoy your vacation and your "Super Senior", then she was laughing out loud when she left.

—My love, I have to pass by my business, do you want to stay or do you want to come with me?

—I will go with you. Give me a few minutes to get dressed.

—Don't take too long!

—They arrived to his business and he introduced her to all the employees as his fiancée and told her that they were a big family at his place. When he met with Richard, he told him:

—I want to talk to you about the business economy. I don't think we are making money, we can only maintain the business and pay the expenses. We are leaving for a few days on vacation, please keep an eye on your sister. I see her light headed. See you soon.

CHAPTER XVII
A VACATION THROUGH THE UNITED STATES

As they were approaching the cabin, Francesca kept looking at the surroundings. It was autumn and the leaves were dry, in multiple colors, among those colors were the browns, reds and yellows and other colors. She was also contemplating all of the animals, such as the deer, the rabbits, the squirrels, the colorful birds and an eagle with a white collar that called her attention.

Christopher stopped the car and told her:

—Look that is an eagle! Since I was young I like those birds, they are probably from this zone.

—How beautiful, she said.

When they arrived to the cabin, they entered and found a mess inside. The refrigerator smelled like if there was a dead animal inside. All furniture and furnishings were covered by dust. Francesca exhaled and sat in a chair looking everywhere and trying to determine where to start cleaning.

—Christopher, please clean the refrigerator. That horrible smell makes me nauseous.

—Don't worry. I am connecting the plant right now. The problem is that in this place there is not electric power or water pipe.

—Then, what do I use to cook?

—Don't worry Francesca, I brought enough water to have extra.

She started cleaning and dusting, then she saw a CD in pieces in the floor next to the record player. She took the pieces and tried to put the CD together. She noticed that it was a CD by Raphael and its title was Francesca, she asked Christopher:

—Love, can you explain what happened to this CD?

—The one that has your name as title, Francesca?

—Was that a reason to destroy it stepping on it?

—At that moment when I heard the song, there was reason. I could have even bitten it if I could have. The rage I felt, yes there was a reason.

They both kept cleaning. He didn't want her to go overboard in her cleaning. A little while ago she told him she was hungry. He responded:

—We will take a shower first and then we eat. I brought lots of canned food.

They went to take a shower and very gently he told her:

—You first, that way the water will be warmer. I am used to bathe in cold water but thinking it over, it is better to take the shower together and that way I receive the double of the heat. When they entered the shower he threw the soap on the floor on purpose and said:

—Francesca, you left the soap fall.

—Really! Do you think I am going to pick it up? You have taken me for a fool many times, but I already know you. You bend and get it.

—No problem. I can bend.

—Yes, you can, but I can't because I don't want to lose my virginity twice.

When Francesca got out of the shower, he dried her body and offered her an apron to wear.

—What kind of cloth are you giving me? Let me get my cloth and I will wear the apron on top.

—No, no, no! Just wear the apron alone. You don't need any more cloth. You look beautiful like this.

She finally went to the kitchen wearing the apron and nothing else. When they were cooking he kept getting closer to her by the back. She turned and told him:

—Oh! I either cook or play. Look at me with the server in my hand. I can defend myself.

—You keep on cooking while I hug you.

—I can't my love, I do either of the two, play or cook. I am extremely hungry and I have to take my pills, go cut the vegetables and help me.

—I can't cut vegetables looking at you naked, I am capable of cutting one of my fingers. Please go and get dressed.

On the way to get clothes to wear Francesca was talking out loud:

—I had never seen this before, it looks like a movie or a burlesque show. Will this always be like that or is it just for some time?

Then he responded:

—Never doubt my love and passion for you, I feel younger every day being with you.

The dinner besides being made of canned food was delicious and they drank Australian wine. It was night time already and they went out and sat in the front porch. The sky was full of stars and little firefly's were flying over Francesca. She was trying to catch them because they caught her attention a lot. She had not seen them since she was a child. Looking around she walked away from the bench, and then right there was a bear standing near her. She screamed so hard that the bear got scare and ran away from her. She ran in panic and almost fell.

—What happened, Francesca?

She couldn't talk, could only scream.

—Get in the Cabin, close all doors and I will tell you later!

—What happened, did you see the devil?

—Oh, oh…worse than that! I had a bear standing next to me.

—Was it? That's normal here every day.

—Snakes passing by my feet? I am not getting out of the cabin anymore. Then Francesca asked:

—Are there frogs here?

—No. Not frogs, toads, big black toads. You can eat them. Do we cook one tomorrow?

—You are crazy. Looks like this vacation will take place inside the Cabin and all dressed up. Is there someone in this place to help in case of emergency?

—Help you, why, from whom? From me? I take care of you like if you were a flower.

—Yes, like a flower that you water all the time with the human sprinkler and with fertilizer.

—Let's listen to some music and rest. I am worried, you have had a difficult day. Did you take your pills? Let's rest. We also enjoy that.

There was a bear walking all around the Cabin and she couldn't sleep with the noise it makes, she spent the night sitting on top of the bed looking through the window. She finally woke Christopher up to ask him if the windows were safe. She told him that she kept seeing red eyes in the woods. He just told her:

—Oh! Those are the wolves.

—Are there also wolves? We would have better gone to Africa.

He got up and took a riffle.

—Where are you going? Don't you dare kill an animal, I am going to feel pain for the animal.

—No, I'm just going to throw two shots into the air to make noise and scare them away. I don't kill animals.

—They woke up late staying in bed until approximately 9:00. Suddenly, Francesca stood up in a jump because she heard steps near the door.

—Francesca, please don't come out in underwear, we have company.

—A visit? At this time?

—It's the sheriff in his round by the cabins.

She got dressed and after Christopher introduced her to the sheriff, who told her that they had known each other for many years. She offered coffee and the Sheriff told her that he had come precisely to have coffee and invite Christopher to go fishing. She jumped:

—Are you going to leave me here alone? Don't even think about that. I am going fishing with you.

The sheriff couldn't understand her English very well and asked her where she was from, she told him that she was French. He also asked Christopher:

—May I ask who she is?

—The woman who will be my next wife.

—Very pretty lady, has very pretty eye color.

—Hey, hey! don't you dare tell my woman anything.

—Wow, I can be your brother!

—Talking about women. How is your wife doing?

—She is splendid, full of grandchildren jumping around the house. After we fish we take the fish to my house and we will eat there. That way your future wife meets mine.

Francesca had never gone fishing and was very excited but she told herself. If I catch one, I will throw it back to the sea. I cannot let it die.

When they arrived to the sheriff's house, she saw a pork leg, and asked:

—What is this?

—Francesca you said we were in Africa. Don't ask and eat.

—I better eat fish.

The women liked each other and were talking for a

long time, but had to stop at intervals because Francesca couldn't understand the other woman well and then Christopher had to interpret for the woman in certain occasions. At approximately 4:00 p.m. Francesca started touching Christopher under the table, telling him.

—Let's go. It's going to be night time pretty soon and we have to walk a lot. You didn't want to bring the truck and you don't want the Sheriff to take me. I want to know if you brought me here to get better or to get rid of me. I am going to be eaten by a bear or a wolf. What if a snake bites me?

—What do you think? There are like 400 families living in this area and none has ever been eaten by an animal. Stop kidding around.

—Please sheriff, convince him and take us back to the cabin. I am in a recovery period because of an accident.

The Sheriff told him:

—Listen Christopher, I am going to take her because there is storm coming this way.

When we got to the cabin the rain started.

—Thank you very much Swheriff!

—Don't worry lady, I will come by tomorrow again.

—Christopher be careful with throwing bullets at night, you are going to scare the neighbors. I knew you were here because you always do that.

—Ok, Sheriff. Don't give me a ticket.

—I cannot even collect a ticket from you.

She went straight to the bathroom to take a shower. Then he told her that the water that was good was the water coming down the roof. He asked her if she had ever taken a shower naked under the rain, he assured her that it is the best shower ever and he invited her to go outside.

—What about the toads and the snakes?

—I showered in Cuba when I was a kid and a couple of times, the first rain in the month of May my mother sent me outside and she told me: *Go take a shower because it is good for the health.* I remember I caught a cold in one of those showers. (He convinced her and they took a shower under the rain).

After the shower they lied down in bed, the rain drops were hitting the roof, the terrace's roof was made of zinc and the drops of rain were hitting hard. He turned towards her and asked her:

—Have you ever made love under a roof made of zinc? With the music of the rain drops hitting the zinc? It is a symphony of tiqui, taca, tiqui, taca. The drops sound like music and we dance in the bed with the patter.

—Is that how you call it now? Pitter, patter.

They were hugging when a lightning hit a tree near the cabin, there was an explosion that lit up the sky. She got nervous, but he made her feel better by asking her not to worry that it was very common in that area and that it was good because it scares the beasts away.

—Looks like your beast is also scared.

Besides the scare, they kept dancing to the pitter patter of the rain. After that they fell asleep. In the morning she jumped and sat on the bed again, because she heard a strong noise outside the cabin. She started calling Christopher but he did not respond. Then she stood up and started looking through the window and then she saw him on top of a lawn mower cutting the grass. She got up, refreshed herself and fixed herself a little and got dressed. She prepared scrambled eggs, toasts, American coffee and orange juice.

Christopher was getting anxious because he didn't know what was going on between Milam and her French guy or how business was. He wanted to talk to his son. After breakfast he asked Francesca to pack because he wanted to take her to another State to be able to get in touch with his family. She was happy to leave but at the same time she felt pain in leaving the cabin so soon. With bears or without bears, this is our first home alone.

She had also experimented new things in her life, they went fishing, saw bears, wolves and beautiful country sites, and besides the savage beasts they had very happy moments. When he came back saw her a little bit melancholic and asked her:

—Do you feel bad?

—Yes and no. It is a sad unknown feeling. I will never forget this cabin and what I have lived in it.

—Well, let's disconnect the plant, the fridge, whatever is left in the fridge we'll take it to the Sheriff on the way. Take a sweater and coat with you because we are going to a very cold State.

—I will also miss the Sheriff and his family!

Trip to New York and the Niagara Falls

On the way from Maryland to New York, they passed through several towns of the United States, trip that they enjoyed together a lot. They had finally arrived to New York. Three days after their arrival to New York they were talking and Christopher asked Francesca:

—Francesca, what has impressed you the most in New York during these days of our stay?

—I liked the Statute of Liberty. It came from my country, it was given as a donation to represent all the immigrants of the world, whom this country gave a warm welcome. I liked Times Square, the Empire State Building, the Central Park and the Science Museum, a lot. And I felt a tremendous sadness when we visited what used to be the Twin Towers where so many people died. Is it true that there are plans to construct two towers taller than this one? Christopher moved his head affirmatively. But, I also enjoyed Fifth Avenue and its shops.

—As you know, we are on our way to the Niagara Falls.

—What a beautiful sight! Nature in autumn in all of its splendor with the mountain bordering the road, what a beautiful trip!, replied Francesca.

Christopher thinking about this trip thought of other happy memories:

We arrived in Buffalo and checked in at a very good hotel, we were tired because of the road trip. The following morning, we woke up, got dressed and chose to be in a group with a guide to visit all of the most important places including the Museum and take the advantage of more stops in less time.

When Francesca saw Niagara Falls she felt very excited and opened her arms as symbol of magnitude and exclaimed:

—Oh! God. What a beautiful place, so much water. Look at the boat down there by the falls, how dangerous!

He explained that there was no danger at all. At that same time, they were going to go down there. They had to go and leave their shoes in a locker and they were given non-slippery shoes and a rain coat. They took a boat with a capacity of hundreds of persons. Christopher took a lot of pictures while she kept saying that she had never seen anything like that. They spent two days at that place and saw the fireworks at night and they had to go back to Maryland, because they were waiting for Camille and her family to arrive any time.

Also, Richard had placed a call to his father, and told him that the situation in the business required his presence and that he had to have a meeting with the accountant.

After the long trip they went back to Maryland and went directly to the house to rest. They were happy but very tired, ate something light and fell asleep almost immediately.

CHAPTER XVIII
ENCOUNTER OF INTEREST

Christopher called a meeting at his office the following morning, with Milam, Richard and the Accountant. When all called to the meeting were there, Richard started talking and told his father that as per the Accountant, the sales had lowered with a little margin of income.

—What do you suggest Richard? The father asked.

—I was talking to the accountant and we came to the conclusion that we need to close some of the branches, since there is no margin of income enough to maintain so many branches in operation.

Christopher felt like traveling in a space ship, he was getting red, seemed like his blood pressure was getting high, and asked:

—Who is the biggest shareholder in this company? Milam, Richard or me? I am the majority holder of the shares, don't I own 51% of the shares? The same for the business as to for the real estate investments, yes or no? OK! Who told you that I am going to fire my employees and close my business? I want to let you have a small resume of the matter. My father in 1948 worked very hard to establish a business and my mother and I were living in a small basement. My mother was working in a factory making pennies, to help my father establish the business. We never heard of vacationing, or a new car or even a good dinner. It was all sacrifice from all of us. Finally, my father was able to establish a gas station as big as those in this town, and I was merely 7 years old when I had to start filling gas tanks without making a penny. I came from school and had to start working with the difficulty of a language that was not ours and besides the inconveniences

we kept going on until we got to be very well off —
Christopher was getting emotional as he spoke—.

We had to leave that country because of the change in
ideology, that intervened our business and we had to start
from zero, here in the United States and with the capacity to
study a career, I had to limit my studies and began working
for my father. Richard, I paid careers for both of you, and
helped you both. You dressed well, ate well and never
lacked anything.

—Dad, you have to understand that we are going through
difficult times in the economy.

—Mr. Accountant, please tell me, are the real estate units
producing the same income or, is there also a deficit in that
business?

—No, Sir. There is profit, not much, but no losses yet. Then,
Christopher talking to Richard:

—I talked to you and explained to you that you and I were
not going to receive a salary and that there was going to be
a cut in the hours of the employees with the result of not
having to fire any employee, don't you remember our
conversation? Your problem is that you were making
approximately $500,000 a year that not even the President
of the United States earns that much. The problem is that I
am positive that you have not saved a penny and you are in
debt now because you have lived like a millionaire. The
best cars, the best boats and other things and you do not
accept this situation. At least your sister has a career, has
invested in real estate and has money in savings.

—Well! I own 24% of the shares in this company, if that
is so, buy my shares.

—What this means is that I gave you 24% of my shares as
a gift so that you could grow and now you sell them to me,
and continued:

—You have disappointed me as a man and as a son.

—Mr. Accountant, please arrange for an appointment with my lawyer, my son, my daughter, you and I, for the transfer of the shares.

—Richard, you have done the same thing that my sister did to my father. She left for New York and left mother, father and home to live the happy life, which contributed to our father's sickness and subsequent death, because he was a very conservative individual.

—Richard, we have spoken. Our relationship ends with the transfer of the shares between father and son, I don't want to see you in my house or in my business, not even as a client, this ends here.

Christopher got up from his desk and went to sit at the terrace, he was very agitated. Milam ran after him and called Francesca. She needed a pill to lower his blood pressure. She asked her maid to locate his family doctor, since she was afraid her father might have a stroke.

Milam kneeled in front of her father and asked him not to take decisions as drastic as that one, to think about it twice, because at this time and under the circumstances, she was not ready to lose her family. To look forward and realize how much he was going to enjoy his granddaughter and while the doctor got there, she kept repeating:

—Dad, please calm down.

She gave him a lime flower tea, while Francesca tried to calm him down without even knowing what was going on. She wanted her step daughter to tell her what was happening.

—Not now, Francesca. I will explain it to you later. The doctor came and found his blood pressure high and asked him to go to the hospital, but Christopher refused, then, the doctor asked his nurse to stay with the patient to check his vital signs and ordered him not to eat any- thing heavy. Only fruits, juices and vegetables and to drink lots of water in the next 24 hours.

The afternoon went by and he was feeling a little bit better and more calmed, but was unable to raise his head and worried about the visitors and the monetary loss. He called Milam and in front of Francesca, he questioned her.

—What is it that your brother spends the money on? Is he using drugs?

—Without a word, Milam moved her head and Christopher realized that what he had said was the reason for the problem.

—Milam why have you not been honest enough to let me know. If you had knowledge that your brother had an addiction, your duty was to inform me. You have both hurt me a lot.

—Dad, what I was trying to avoid was adding more suffering on top of those we already know.

—Well, I now have two problems instead of one. I will not pay him a penny for his shares, he has to give them back to me even if I have to take him to court. I don't intend to give him more money to invest it in his own destruction and ours, daughter, please call him and ask him not to show up at the business anymore, that I will be in charge of everything and to attend counseling to fight addictions.

Camille and her family arrived from France the following day, right in the middle of this catastrophe. He didn't demonstrate it but he thought it was a bad timing for them to come and visit. He asked Milam to take care of Richard and Camille's family, because he did not have time or strength to face so many problems. He asked her to hire an agency to take them to different places in the United States and the last stop in Walt Disney World in Florida, so that the child could enjoy the trip. The days went by, Francesca had to accompany them in the trip to Disney because the little girl insisted on her going and Christopher told her that there was no problem for her to go, on the contrary, it would be better because he was too concentrated on the business matters. Besides that, he had initiated an investigation through a private detective to find out who were Richard's friends and who was the person that was providing or selling his son drugs.

The investigation showed that in fact Richard was contacting a person in a Baltimore's low class neighborhood that provided him with the drug at a very high price. Christopher had already contacted a specialist in detoxification of drugs and that as he suspected, lack of money was one of the primary symptoms of addiction.

Since he still had his capital, he contacted a famous clinic because he had been told that said institution was one of the best in treatment of addictions in the country. Christopher arranged for an appointment with the clinic and assistance was immediately granted, considering the fact that his investigations showed that it was a case where immediate attention was necessary because the patient was addicted to cocaine. He also inquired as to how long the rehabilitation of an inpatient would take. The Counselor told him that it depended on the patient's needs, but it usually takes 30 to 90 days as an inpatient. The center was located in Minnesota, a state rather far from Maryland.

Christopher contacted Richard and asked him to meet him in his office as soon as possible to let him know about certain extremely important affairs. Richard was a little bit afraid when he arrived at his father's house because he thought it had to do with the big extractions of money he had made from the business for his personal use. When they finally met, Christopher told him:

—Hi! son, please come in.

—How do you feel Dad?

—How can I feel? when a drug addiction is destroying your life and also those of our family and those of many employees, because this is also affecting our business.

—How did you get to that conclusion? Who made up that story?

—It is not a comment or story. I can show you a report from a private investigator that I hired to follow your steps because you are not the same person anymore. I have the name of the person who provides you with the drugs, a certain William Scott. You meet with this man up to three times a week. I also have pictures of your meetings with that man. Let me tell you, I have an audit forthcoming and I wouldn't like same to show embezzlement in our accounts by others, it is better for you to tell me the truth and it will be between you and I. I will replace from my own capital whatever sum you took because the auditor if it is a considerable sum of money, will inform the authorities.

—Where do you want to take this father?

—Wherever I want as long as I can rehabilitate you from this addiction that is destroying you. I would rather see you in prison than destroyed and wandering through the streets like a homeless person because of this addiction, having lost all of the constitutional rights and not being able to recover your position in this business.

—I will stop when I want.

—I don't believe that. You choose, the audit in front of authorities or rehab in one of the best centers in the United States. Maybe it will only take a period of 30 days depending on your progress and your interest in this rehabilitation. In the meantime, let me tell you that all of your personal belongings are coming this way and you will not get out of this house until you go to the Rehabilitation Center. Your friend is already on his way to prison.

—Anything else, dad?

—No, go to your room that I need to give this issue some rest. I have even gotten my wife and her family out of this house for me to be able to put you back in your place.

Time elapsed and approximately 70 days after that conversation had passed, Christopher, Francesca and Milam, who was seven months pregnant were on their way to Minnesota. They were going to get Richard. Milam asked her father:

—Dad, please tell me the truth, do you believe that Richard is completely rehabilitated?

—According to the clinic's staff, he is another person. That doesn't mean that I am not going to be on top of him all the time. I have a Christian Study waiting for him.

They picked him up at the Clinic. He hugged his sister and tears came out of his eyes as he did.

—Father, there is something I need to tell you. First of all, that I have a great father, that I will be eternally grateful to you for taking me to this Center, I have met very good persons in this place who had also been driven this low and I found Christ through a Christian Counselor who has become my friend and taught me the ways of faith, I am already in contact with a priest near my home and I will start taking Bible lessons, to be able to help other persons with addictions.

—I had plans to take you to a Christian Center but you had already taken the lead —said Christopher— you look more handsome and more of a man.

—Father, I also need to start a family like yours, this is

your second time around, but, you have made a good choice again.

Tears came out of Francesca's eyes, Milam looked at her and also cried. Then, Richard to stop that sentimental moment told Milam.

—Hey Milam what a big belly, you are almost ready to deliver the child!

—No brother, I have two more months to go, but, I have not found out about the child's sex, because I want it to be a surprise, but if it's a boy I will name him Richard to continue my father's tradition and if it is a girl I will name her Marie after the Virgin Mary and Angelina because of the father's mother. Christopher looked at her and asked: Who is the father?

—Pierre, the man who chose this child to be his since the beginning.

—Who is Pierre? Asked Richard.

—You know him. The man who went to meet my dad at his business and had dinner with us.

—Oh! The handsome French guy?

—Milam, my child, he is still in France.

—Don't worry. He will be here anytime. He is pending only one letter from the Immigration Department.

Francesca is leaving soon to France, said Christopher, to take care of some Immigration issues, because her daughters, Camille and Chloe are coming to the United States in capacity of investors, because the economy in France is very bad. I have taken care of all of the necessary documentation required by Immigration and they shall be arriving very soon, since they are not coming as immigrants.

Then Richard said:

—Please dad, don't bring a pretty French Girl for me.

—Not French son. They only woman that will put you in place is a Cuban Woman.

—He is crazy, I want an American Girl to work with me in the missions after I have become a Priest.

—Son! I wonder if you already left that American Girl in the Center.

—You are right, but she is not a patient. She is a nurse.

—I am glad. When do we meet her?

—Very soon.

CHAPTER XIX
ARRIVAL OF FRANCESCA AND HER FAMILY TO THE USA INDEFINITELY

The wedding of Christopher and Francesca had already taken place in the French Riviera. Both families were present and there was a small celebration in France in a Restaurant because they were planning to take a trip on their first wedding anniversary.

Eighteen months had passed and all of Francesca's family arrived to the United States. They had all obtained the status of permanent residents in the United States. Milam had married Pierre and had a beautiful daughter who is sixteen months old. Richard married and his wife is pregnant, (with his own church); Yanay and her policeman were also visiting. They are not coming to stay because Yanay inherited Francesca's business. Francesca wanted to keep her apartment on top of the Boutique because she has it as a remembrance of her relationship with Christopher.

—She had never said she was getting rid of her apartment, whenever I visit my apartment, I see it in mind covered with rose petals and we have champagne waiting for us. I am a very fortunate woman, not all women have the capacity of loving this much, like I do.

When they arrived to Christopher's house, Guadalupe was walking Marie Angelina, because she was her nana now and she had two other women to take care of the house, because the family had grown.

The baby ran, first to her grandfather and then to her parents.

—Grandpa, grandma! She screamed, and kissed them.

Francesca carried the baby and then Milam said:

—I hope that this child we are expecting, comes to us first.

—Milam, are you expecting again? Asked Christopher.

—Yes, and very proud. Here comes the new Richard and Pierre is the best man I could have ever picked as a father.

Richard, smiling answers his sister:

—On top of being a good father, confess, you picked him because he was good looking. Let me tell you, Alexa, my wife, is giving birth before you do, and if a boy, we are naming him Richard and if it is a girl, she will name her after her.

—Then I will name mine Pierre and if another girl, I will name her Katherine, like my mother.

Yanay jumps and says:

—Since I was jealous, I am also pregnant, if it is a girl, we will name her Francesca, and if it's a boy we will name him Prince, if his father agrees. This love story has gotten very deep into me.

On the first wedding anniversary, Christopher and Francesca left to celebrate in a cruise through the Caribbean Seas and visited Cozumel, Grand Cayman and Ocho Rios and the private Bahama Island. When they passed by Cuba they both got nostalgic, then exhaling she told her husband:

—When will I be able to come back to Cuba again? Or better, when will we be able to come?

—The Americans cannot visit Cuba yet, maybe in the future when some of the differences disappear. I promise you that you and I will be the first to come, said Christopher.

They could drink all they wished in the Cruise, because they didn't have to drive, in an occasion, Christopher and Francesca "drank a lot." When they went to the cabin, Christopher tried carrying her, but between the alcohol, the age and some weight that Francesca had gained by that time he couldn't do it and almost fell at the entrance of the cabin. They were both laughing out loud. They could be heard from the hall. "They were too drunk." Once inside the cabin he jumped on top of the bed completely dressed and with shoes on and said in a loud voice: "Here is your Tarzan, come over Jane".

Since Francesca was more sober than him, said:
—We are only missing Cheeta. Someone knocked on the door, and he screamed. There is "Cheeta."

Francesca opened the door and told the kid that knocked. We are fine. Come back tomorrow, everything is in order. When she was turning back from the door she heard something hitting the bed, she ran scared. She found Christopher snoring on top of the bed all dressed and his shoes still on. She was a lot smaller and couldn't hardly undress him and take his shoes off, but she finally did it, she was sweating when she was done. She sat by him, grabbed his cheek and told him:
—Tarzan. What an anniversary you are giving me. Seems like I am going to bed by myself and you snoring. I will make you pay for this tomorrow. Don't worry!

The following morning, they couldn't celebrate either, because the hang over and the head ache they both had, was horrible. They were not used to drink alcoholic beverages and that made things worse. The following days when they felt better, were fulfilled with strawberries and chocolate, caviar and champagne, (warm and cold), and rose petals. That way they reconstructed their past, without family affairs, just Christopher and Francesca.

CHAPTER XX
DREAM TRIP

The Smith's house is dressed up in a very luxurious Birthday Party! Christopher and Francesca are turning 70 with a month's difference between them and their children organized a big party to surprise them, most of the persons invited were the more intimate, but also there were several old employees, the lawyer, the accountant, a priest and a Catholic priest, as well as some political representatives.

Christopher and Francesca found out about the party when they got to the house, they saw a red rug running through the entrance of the house where an arc of flowers was placed. They were coming back from a trip of three days from Washington because Francesca wanted to visit the museums to celebrate her birthday. It was nearly 7:00 at night when they arrived and upon arriving he said:

—Hey! Who is getting married now? It seems like the wedding is going to be late because no one has arrived yet. How strange is this all! Are we in the right house?

Francesca responded:

—This is our house, look at the number, this is it!

When they introduced the key, there was a loud noise and there was an orchestra lead by violins that started playing one of Christopher's favorite songs "My Way", which song he loved interpreted by Frank Sinatra. They also played favorite songs interpreted by Paul Anka, Lionel Richie and Andrea Boccelli among other famous interpreters of romantic songs from the years of the 50's and 60's, all the way through 2016. The songs were changing in accordance with the years they had lived. Everyone was dressed in Gala outfits, the visitors, the family and even the grandchildren were wearing Gala outfits.

Immediately after their arrival, Guadalupe, Yanay and Chloe took Francesca to take a shower, then helped her do her makeup and they fixed her hair. Yanay had designed and had made the most beautiful Gala Dress for her.

On the other hand, Richard took his dad upstairs and gave him a tuxedo from a famous designer, shiny shoes and a set of a bow for the neck and handkerchief, as a personal gift from Richard. Christopher took a shower and got dressed he looked like an Emperor.

—Hey, dad! My old man, do you want a hat and a walking stik?

—Hey, Richard. Do you think I am an old man?

—No, dad. You are only a wasted "Super Senior". You don't fly or run. I have another gift for you.

—Please remember that I don't wear jewelry.

—Open the gift, this jewelry will do a lot for you tonight.

When Christopher opened the box, found a couple of blue pills inside.

—How wrong you are. I don't need that.

—Well, I have heard rumors about you needing help.

—Let's leave this conversation here and go back to the party.

They went to the ball room and the orchestra was playing Paul Anka's Song "Put your Head on my Shoulder". Christopher looked at Francesca and he was astonished to see her beauty. He saw her as the first time he went to the theater with her, ten years ago.

—How beautiful you look, my love.

He took her in his arms and started dancing with her.

—You too. Prince of my dreams. You look beautiful and look like you are in your thirties.

This was the second time the same song was played. The grandchildren made a circle around their grandparents when the cake was going to be cut, immense and with 70 handles. At that moment they sang the "Happy Birthday" and the kids blew the candles. They were dancing, eating and dancing to that beautiful music until midnight. The children brought the gifts to them, among which there were two wrist watches with little diamonds in the spheres. Yanay bought a "Guayabera" for Christopher and a typical Cuban country dress for Francesca. Angeline the eldest grandchild while the Orchestra was playing a music fit for a surprise gift, gave them a sealed envelope.

—Well, dad, there are two plane tickets in that envelope —said Milam—. Guess where you are going to celebrate your 70's.

Francesca started guessing and said:

—I cannot think of a place that we can visit that we have not seen, there are a very few places which we have not gone.

Milam then talking to her father said:

—Ok Dad. We all met and got to a decision that this is what you both have been waiting to see for a long time.

—Oh! I believe I already know where we are going and in a low voice he told Francesca, it has to be Cuba.

—It can't be.

Let me ask my daughter.

—Are there tobaccos, guayaberas, expresso, Rum, rice, black beans, Yuca and baked pork?

—Yes, dad. You got it.

—When are we leaving?

—You are leaving in 10 days. You have to go to Miami to take the flight. It is a 21-day trip, go and rest from this tribe that loves you very much.

—Dad, don't leave the Blue Virgin. That one revives the dead —said Richard.

—What Virgin is this kid talking about?

—Francesca, my father will answer your question and will show you the Virgin in your room.

—Christopher was doubtful thinking about that but didn't say anything.

Francesca was thinking about that for a minute and then said:

—Richard, I thought about it and I know what Blue Virgin you are talking about. Let me tell you that you are wrong.

—Go for it Francesca, said Christopher.

—Listen kid. This is my Tarzan and I am his Jane.

—Then I am Cheeta.

They went to bed, but he called his doctor from the room and the doctor asked him:

—Yes, Christopher. Is there a problem?

—No, no, doctor. I am sorry to call you so late.

—What can I do for you?

—Can I take a pill, doctor? —and whispered the name of the pill to the doctor.

—Well. If your blood pressure is fine, you can take a little piece of the pill. If it is too low you can't, you can have a problem. Honestly, just because it is you I answered this late. You are my friend. If, not I would have sent you to hell.

—As far as Alaska?

—I can't do that to you.

He took the pill and cut it into three pieces and took a piece of wine from one of two cups they had waiting for them in the room. They talked about the party for approximately 30 minutes. They talked about their children and other people. Then, Christopher told her he was going to put some music on, soft and romantic music. Let's remember our romantic moments in France. Then he put a song to dance together.

—All my Life, Sang by Linda Wonstand and Aaron Nevil. Am I really here in your arms?

—It is just as I dreamed it would be, I feel like we are frozen in time and you are the only one I see. Hey! I have looked for you all my life.

They were dancing together very close to each other and all of a sudden she told him.

—Hey! What is that touching my body? She lowered the hand and touched him

—What is going on here?

—What's wrong my love?

—No. Nothing, nothing. Take your cloth off and then we'll dance. Please Christopher, take your cloth off!

—Why do women get so fancy. Why don't you take your's off too? Am I the only one to undress this time?

—No problem. I will take mine off now.

He took his clothes off and looked down. He was definitely surprised at the sight.

—What is this? Not even when I was thirty years old.

She had taken her cloth off and turned to him and when she saw him she was very surprised and kept telling him:

—Oh my God! What is this? I have finally met Tarzan. No problem, Jane is here.

—The Blue Virgin is a real miracle.

— It has been a little dead lately —said Francesca.

—Are you also making a joke of this? Like Richard.

They started dancing and she asked him to go to bed before the effect of the pill was gone.

They spent a long time together in bed. They enjoyed the bed and forced themselves to demonstrate their passion for each other just as at the beginning of their relationship for many years. He had gone to take a shower and looking down to his complete body:

—Wow. You are still alive!

Francesca was already sleeping and he started screaming to her from the bathroom:

—Francesca, look here. This is your Tarzan!

She looked thinking that she was tired but had to take advantage of the pill.

—Here is your Jane! (in a very weak voice).

They went back to bed and battled until the soldier died. Then, they went to sleep.

The following morning, Christopher called his son to tell him that he was very grateful for the party and the surprise, but, to specifically tell him how happy he was with the Blue Virgin. Richard then asked him if he had enjoyed the pill.

—Until the morning. (Christopher responded). Richard said:

—Hey! I will get one too. It doesn't hurt.

—If you use it, have only a small piece. That is enough. If not, you can have a health issue. When you buy yours, please get me some for the trip.

—We are leaving sooner to spend a few days in Florida. I want to have a two-day trip in Florida and then we will go to Cuba, I have friends in Miami and I will leave the car with them so that I can use it on the way back.

They went to Cape Canaveral to see the space Museum. Then they went to St. Augustine, where they spent the night and visited Sea World in Orlando where they stayed at a nearby hotel, on the way to Miami they stopped at Marco Island and spent two days in Marco Island and they liked it so much that decided to get information about real estate investments in that place. They loved the town and found it very relaxing for older people and liked the Tropical Climate without the snow storms, earthquakes or forest fires. They saw it as a paradise.

The last stop was Miami Beach where they stayed at the Fountainblue Hotel and enjoyed the beach, the Parrot Jungle and some Museums. Another place of interest was Little Havana and they felt like if they were in Cuba. All signs in Spanish. Saw Coral Gables, also a beautiful place with all the streets named in Spanish. They asked a man standing in the sidewalk at S.W. 8th Street in Miami for a good Cuban Restaurant and the man advised them that there were lots of Cuban Restaurants in 8th Street, that many Presidents when visiting Miami had stopped to eat in Eight Street. They told the man that they were very grateful for his advice. When they got to a Cuban Restaurant they felt very comfortable and saw so many Cuban Dishes that didn't know which one to pick. They finally ate what they remembered the most: Baked pork, rice, black beans, yucca, Avocado Salad, Wine and Cuban Coffee. As they ate tears came down their cheeks. The waitress saw them a little old and asked them if they were fine. Francesca said yes, this food brings many remembrances to us.

—Are you Cuban?

—As if we were! We spent our childhood in Cuba.

CHAPTER XXI
TRIP TO CUBA

It was finally time to arrive to the Miami International Airport to take the flight to Cuba. They were both nervous because more than fifty years had passed since they left Cuba.

They took an itinerary that their children prepared for them. They have made all the reservations and tours for them. Before they arrived to Havana they were looking down from the plane. They could see many different shades of green, the soil was red in some areas, lots of Palm Trees and the incomparable shape of the Island. The airplane finally descended in the "Jose Marti International Airport".

They took a taxi that took them to "Hotel Nacional". During the trip both looked through the windows of the car looking for memories as well as new buildings. When they arrived to the Hotel, found it beautiful and restored. This was a very famous hotel which had for guests very famous Artists, Presidents as well as Members of the Mafia. They rested that day without leaving the place. They had gone through many remembrances and emotions. They felt very tired and Francesca had a head-ache. She used to live in Havana all the time until she left and went back to France.

The following morning, they had breakfast at the hotel and then Francesca asked her husband to go for a walk by "El Malecón" (a wall to restrain the sea to come into the City), very beautiful place for a walk. Later that day they took a taxi to look around Old Havana, they passed by The Capitol, The Rampa (a very tall building) The Cathedral and many famous hotels, restaurants (such as Sloppy Joe's, a very world famous cafeteria) and theaters. The imitation of the Famous Paris Lord (Caballero de

Paris), Havana BayTunnel (which brought many remembrances to Francesca), they saw the Cemetery of Colon (One of the most important and beautiful cemeteries Worldwide). They went back to the Hotel, it was night already, they were tired; had dinner at the restaurant in the Hotel, since they didn't want to walk anymore. After dinner they passed by the Cabaret.

The next morning, Francesca wanted to drive by her school, the house she lived in and the Hotel where her father worked. She visited the Hotel and asked a lot of people if they had known her father. She used to live in a pretty high class neighborhood. Since she arrived to Havana, she was thinking about her old house all the time.

Francesca was able to see her house and her school. It was all very well kept because the properties were restored. The Hotel where her father worked had also been restored. Many memories.

Very early the following morning they went to "Pinar del Rio" the Province in the extreme Occidental part of Cuba. They went in a luxurious touristic bus with a guide that spoke perfect English, besides the Spanish. They passed by the Tobacco market place (which neither of them had seen before). They rolled tobacco for Christopher right in front of him. He smoked it but it made Francesca dizzy. He was euphoric and kept saying:

—This is a real tobacco, but had to throw it away before getting onto the bus.

They visited the Viñales Valley also in Pinar del Rio. They kept looking through the window of the bus contemplating the different shades of green in the Valley, the beautiful sight of the countryside of Cuba. Also, kept living memories of their childhood in Cuba, since that they had never visited those places, they were amazed. They spent an hour in the valley balcony and later on, also visited "La Cueva del Indio", a very special place for the Aborigines. They went in a boat through the subterranean river. When it was late afternoon the bus took them back to the Hotel. They were very tired but took a shower and went to dance Cuban and American Music. They danced to Caribbean Music and also to an American dance by a singer named Billy Ocean, the name of the song was "Caribbean Queen". Then, also danced to the Famous Cuban Orchestra "Aragon" and a world known dance "Cha, cha, cha" by Nat King Cole. They were exhausted by midnight and went straight to bed, they couldn't even take their cloth off.

Nostalgic, they said bye to Havana leaving first thing in the morning the following day. They were taken by the Tunnel of the Bay of Havana and took the road called the Monumental Road and then later the Via Blanca, the road that goes to the Province of Matanzas. They were going to Varadero Beach. They passed by the Bacunayagua Bridge, the tallest bridge in Cuba and had lunch at the Bridge's balcony or window. The sight was impressive and the food was delicious. It was seasoned Cuban style. They commented that they had not eaten so well-seasoned in years.

Varadero Beach. One of the most beautiful beaches in the world with its white sand that makes its waters transparent. They took many pictures and went fishing. Francesca had never fished in the sea. She was very hyper, doing things she had never done. They were so enthusiastic that they forgot to use sun block or protection for the skin. They looked like shrimps. They were thinking about the shrimps and how they looked and went to a bar to eat seafood. All that Christopher wanted was shrimps and a very cold beer. Francesca seemed like a little girl enjoying her trip, wearing beach clothes and sun glasses. She looked very pretty and you could tell that they were tourists.

They walked in the sand and after looking at some hotels they took a carriage with horses to go to Varadero City and all through the city, they were holding hands and kissing like two adolescents and enjoying the breeze that came from the sea. It was an unforgettable passage that they would remember many years after that when they were holding hands.

They went back to the hotel to change and go dancing again, but, they were late to the dance because they spent a lot of time enjoying each other's company in the hotel room. Their bodies were so hot that could hardly touch their skin because of the sunburn. They stayed late dancing but had to retired to the room because their feet were hurting and it felt like people in their 70's for the first time. The next day, they took a bus to visit Cayo Coco Beach. The beach was very similar to Varadero but it was a key in the middle of the sea in front of the Bahamas. The Gulf of Mexico and the Atlantic Ocean meet in those waters. The beach had very nice places to stay, very unusual little houses by the sea. They stayed three days in Cayo Coco Beach and then decided to go on their own to the City of Matanzas. Francesca had only been to Varadero. Christopher lived 12 years in Matanzas.

—My love —he told Francesca—. Let me show you the places where I lived and was brought up. First, the Yumuru Valley that I used to visit in bicycle with a group of friends. We used to eat Mangoes and catch crabs to eat. Second, the Statute at the Liberty Park where the young people used to meet; third the San Juan River where I swam and jumped from the bridge, behind the backs of my parents. The house where we lived. The Beyamar Caves also famous worldwide because of its Stalactites and Stalagmites that some of them form animal figures and other things, then the Sauto Theater that was also used as a Movie Theater. We will now go to another part of the City that I want you to see.

When they were in the Caves when it was very dark, the guide told them. You can use this darkness to kiss. He took advantage of the situation and introduced his hand under her shorts. She rapidly turned very mad thinking it had been another tourist who touched her. She was mad when she told him:

—You don't miss the opportunity to introduce your hand inside my clothes. I got very scare, wait until I get you by surprise! What compensates this trip underground is the beauty of this place.

He took her to his father's gas station and showed her most of the places where he spent his infancy. Sometimes his eyes got watery almost ready to cry, thinking about his father. Francesca noticed how emotional he was feeling.

The next day they went on a tour through all the rest of the Island, Camaguey and Oriente. They saw Water Falls, Mountains, Sugar Mills, many beaches, museums, many beautiful churches, including the "Sanctuary of Virgin of Charity", Cuban Patron, located in "Oriente". They spent six days in this sightseeing tour. Cuba is very beautiful.

They went back to Havana and stayed at the same hotel, they took two days to rest before going back to the United States. Francesca proposed the following to Christopher:

—My love, this is our last night in Havana. I am going to

ask you several things. Can you grant them? He answered fast:

—When is it that I have denied something to my princess?

—First. I want to move to Florida, Marco Island. I am tired of the snow. You and I suffer from arthritis and that is an ideal place for my Super Senior and for me. What do you think about this first proposal?

—Yes. It sounds good. When we get home we have to talk to Milam, who is a Real Estate Agent and can find a big apartment for us facing the sea, so that our children and grandchildren can spend their vacations with us.

She proceeded asking:

—Do you have any of the blue pills left?

He answered:

—What do you want those pills for?

—What would I want the pill. It is for my Tarzan.

—Hey princess. Do not get addicted to that pill. What do you think? That pill is not for every day. You were very quiet, but you came out of the Pandora Box 10 years ago and don't lose your energy. Instead of me having one of those pills, why don't I give you a sleeping pill?

—Hey Christopher!, instead of giving me a sleeping pill why don't you get a pump?

—Hey Francesca! My love, why don't you realize that we are 70 years old?

—OK, Christopher, if you don't want to take the pill, why don't we kiss?

—Yeahhhhhhhhhhhhhhhh!

OBSERVATIONS TO THE READER

This book is a love story. The authors have tried to introduce in some of the chapters, a picaresque tone, always within the parameters of respect. Some other Chapters can result passionate because it talks about the intimate relationship of a couple that finds the opportunity to be happy when they did not expect it. We have tried to not violate moral standards, we have only tried to make the book more pleasant.

It has several family situations, counseling and everyday life experiences.

Any resemblance of any of the characters in this book with persons in real life is pure coincidence.

I hope that you enjoy this book as much as we have, we have laughed, cried and have lived memorable times. One of the authors, Humberto Paez, has written three other books. We thank you for letting us come into your homes or wherever you choose to read. *Humberto Paez and Carmen Castellanos Soto*

INDEX

Made in the USA
Columbia, SC
20 November 2021

49331882R00114